If the Gods be Willing

The Cold Death, Volume 1

Taylor Metzler

Published by Taylor Metzler, 2024.

IF THE GODS BE WILLING

First edition. May 24, 2024.

Copyright © 2024 Taylor Metzler.

ISBN: 979-8224642144

Written by Taylor Metzler.

To my Dad, who helped me discover the love of books.

To my children, for putting up with me while I wrote this.

To my husband, who pushed me hard enough to get this done.

Chapter 1

Fall sun thrums down on a busy marketplace in Dion, Greece. The air is rich in both aroma and sound as it streams around Cassia, a slender, aged woman dressed in flowing, brightly colored clothes. She weaves her way deftly through the crowds. Her olive brown skin glows under the warm sun and inside, she is happy.

She pops into a booth to pick up a couple pounds of ground lamb, then another for tomatoes, aubergines, and kefalotyri cheese. At each booth she doles out hugs, laughing, to the occupants. By the time she's done, she also has a bottle of red wine, a basket of dolmades, and a ring of sesame-coated koulouri, all given gratis.

When her grocery list has been completed, Cassia enters a temple-booth to Asclepius to pray. Inside the tent flaps is a small waiting room with an attendant on duty. She smiles at him.

"Anastasios!" she exclaims. "How are you? How is your wife doing? I heard she had the baby finally."

He nods. "Yes, just after I saw you last week, actually. My oldest boy came running all the way in to town to fetch me."

"And? Girl or boy this time?"

"Another boy." He shrugs shyly.

"What's that make? Six boys now?"

"You have the math correct, Cassia. It's so kind of you to remember."

"Well, you always remember Haris' birthday, too. It's what we do, Anastasios. This isn't just a town, it's a community."

"You are right. As always," he says, smiling.

"Well, I should get inside and make my prayers so I can help Sophie with lunch. It won't make itself. Say hi to Penelope for me, and the wee one."

"I will. And you to Sophie, and Haris if you see him. He's away at college, right?"

"Well, 'away' is a loose term. It's just a city over. But yes, he has his own place now, so that's lovely."

They hug quickly, then she turns to the interior door.

Inside the magical space, it feels cooler by at least twenty degrees, more like a mountain temple than the middle of Dion's busy marketplace. On the pedestal next to the entrance is a canister of pins. She sets her bags down and takes one. She pricks her finger and, finding her blood red, drops it into the bin at her feet. Affixing a prepared bandage to stop the bleeding, she proceeds further. It is easier to breathe with the sounds of the marketplace muffled. The room is bigger than one would expect from the outside, with stone walls and floors and the slow dripping of water. Snakes intertwine around the columns and there's a statue of Asclepius as a bearded middle-aged man in the center. Kneeling down on a plush red rug in front of a wall fountain of clear water filtering down, she cups her palms and fills them with water from the fountain, then brings it up and over her brown curls. Her voice is low as she intones her obeisance.

"Oh Asclepius, greatest of physicians, I beseech you to protect Sophie, even though she doesn't attend your temple. She lacks faith, my Lord, but not heart; and Haris, for he lacks time but not faith. Both have good hearts and are my world, and what they lack in attendance they make up for with good deeds. Please keep them healthy and safe from the freezing disease. I ask only for them, not for myself, as I know you bestow only so many benedictions. Thank you, Asclepius."

She collects her purchases as she exits the serenity of the asclepia, flowing easily back into the frenzy of the marketplace. Sweat coalesces instantly in all the various crevices of her body, despite the loose clothes she wears. Her hair begins to dry, but will be plastered to her head by the time she gets home. She zigzags between the booths again, and voices call out to her as she passes. Some know her and seek her attention. Others wish only for her coin, as it is clear from her attire that she has it in abundance. She barely acknowledges them, her mind set now on returning home. She enjoys a bite of the koulouri, savoring the crunchy outside paired with the soft inside. She saves the dolmades for lunch with Sophie.

She turns a corner and there is her home, nestled between two other buildings. It's tall and narrow, with flowering vines trailing down the walls, and windows open to admit laughter. Cassia smiles. Haris must be home; it's good to hear Sophie sound so happy. Inside, the downstairs is not much more than a coat closet. Cassia sheds her sandals and untangles herself from her satchel, then ascends the stairs quickly, even more eager now to arrive. She walks into the kitchen; this is the room with the wide-open windows. There are plants everywhere, spider plants and a money tree and lilies and even a philodendron, all in full bloom.

The laughter and voices trail in through an arched entryway. She peeks around the corner, into the dining room. At the table sit Sophie, her skin pale and her nose crooked in the middle, with deep laugh lines around her blue eyes, and Haris, whose heartbreaker smile will one day etch laugh lines to match his mothers'. They are in such deep conversation they don't notice Cassia come in. Mellow afternoon sunlight streams in through the window, bringing out the red streaks in their strawberry blonde hair. Sophie's weathered hands cradle Haris's soft ones, her pale skin against his slightly darker skin, and Cassia wonders what it is that brought him here today. She doesn't intrude, instead quietly walking back into the kitchen and putting away her haul from the marketplace. She starts making lunch. She decides to save the moussaka for dinner – she is hungry and doesn't want to wait. Instead, she pulls out some leftover chicken to make some quick gyros. As she chops the meat, she overhears snippets; "...she said I was too..." and "...I thought she was the..."; enough to gather that his latest girlfriend must have broken up with him.

"Ah, to be 21 and dating again," she thinks, seriously pondering the concept. She shakes her head like she's trying to rid it of a spider. "No, I'm glad I'm not."

"Is that you, Cassia?" Sophie calls out.

Too late she realizes she spoke the last sentence louder than she'd meant to. "Yes, my love. I'm about done making lunch." She plates the food without any eye for appearance – that's more Sophie's thing. But they'll still be tasty.

"Did you see Haris is here?"

"Yes, my love. Hi, Haris," she says as she walks into the dining room, balancing the three plates of food and the basket of dolmades before depositing them on the table. She gives him a quick peck on the cheek, then a longer kiss for Sophie.

"Ew, do you guys have to?" Haris whines and grabs a plate of food.

They laugh quietly and break their kiss. Cassia touches her forehead to Sophie's and their eyes meet with a promise.

"One would think you'd know all about this by now, Haris," Cassia teases, sitting down on the bench next to Sophie and taking her hand. "What with being 21 and all. Still can't handle your moms kissing, eh?"

"Ugh, Mitéra!"

"Okay, okay, I'll stop. It's good to see you, Haris, for any reason. I take it things didn't go well with... Esther?"

"Claudia. But no, things didn't go well. She broke up with me at that fancy restaurant you suggested I propose to her at."

"I didn't suggest you propose! I simply said that's where I took your mom after I proposed to her. Did she break up with you before or after you proposed?"

"After." He sighs and buries his head in his hands. Muffled, he continues. "She said I'm too needy. That it was too quick."

"How long had you been together?"

"Six months!" He almost shouts, then gets quiet. "That's a long time! Isn't it?"

Cassia shrugs and Sophie snickers. "For some, it is, and others it isn't."

"You two were only together a month! How did you know that Mom was the one, that she'd say yes?"

Cassia shrugs again. "I didn't know she'd say yes. But I knew the moment I saw her I'd never love anyone else again. Waiting a whole month dating her felt like torture, when all I wanted to do was get married, move in together and start a family. But I didn't want to scare her off..."

Cassia and Sophie share a smile, remembering.

A moonlit night, a quartet playing a kantada, at a party by the ocean, too many people but even so, two pairs of eyes meet across the expanse, and like the gravitational pull of a meteorite to earth, are pulled toward each other, orbiting and finally colliding.

"Hi," the Greek one says. "I'm Cassia."

"Hi," the American one whispers. "I'm Sophie."

And so, it began.

Chapter 2

Cassia stands at the balcony doors, looking out across the rooftops through sheer blue curtains. The city at night seems a different beast than the one during the day, its lines softer and more nuanced. Some windows have light streaming out, from a candle or a gas lamp, but most of the city is cloaked in darkness. She likes to imagine the lives going on behind curtains, past closed doors. Are her neighbors happy? What are their struggles? She sighs, and turns to pick up a glass of Moscato from the side table. Her nightgown flows with her as she moves, its white lace delicate. She's had this nightgown for something like thirty years, having picked it up not long after she and Sophie got married. She sits down in the armchair by the window and sips at her wine.

Sophie enters from the bathroom, carrying a small gas lamp and setting it down on the bedside table. Its soft light reflects off her light pink silk pajamas. She watches Cassia for a few moments, love in her eyes. Finally, she speaks softly. "So... Dating me was torture, eh?"

Cassia looks up from her reverie and smiles as she takes in Sophie. "Yes and no. Waiting to marry you was torture. The dating part was nice enough, as dating goes. I have enjoyed making a life with you far more."

Sophie smiles, leans against the bed post. "Good answer. You always know how to charm me. Tell me more."

"I never did care for the rush of dating, the anxiety of whether they liked me. I have enjoyed greatly spending our days together, the miracle of the Gods giving us a son together, and watching him grow up with the best and worst of us both. I wouldn't trade it for any of the excitement of dating."

Sophie nods in understanding. "I think that's what Haris wants. He's seen us be so happy together. He craves that deep connection we have. Did we do a disservice to him somehow?"

Cassia sighs and drinks the last few sips, then sets the empty glass down on the side table. "You don't have to second guess every parenting move or decision, my love. He'll find the one he's looking for eventually."

"How do you know for sure?"

"Because, like him, I once craved that deep connection, that bond, and I thought I'd never find it. But I did. I have found my one love." She crosses the room to Sophie.

"And what do you intend to do with her?" Sophie asks, coy.

She trails her fingers lightly up Sophie's bare arm to her shoulder, up her neck, along her jaw and finally ending at her lips. "Kiss her senseless, obviously."

Sophie moans against Cassia's mouth. When they break the kiss, she asks breathlessly, "Is that it?"

"Not nearly." Cassia leans in and kisses Sophie again, deeper this time. She runs her fingers through Sophie's thick hair, then trails her lips down her neck. Sophie moans as Cassia reaches the top button of her pajama top, slowly unbuttoning it and revealing bare skin beneath. She nips at Sophie's neck, then trails down, down between her breasts, across her belly button, to the edge of her pants. She stops and looks up, her dark eyes hooded, and asks, "Do you want me to stop?"

"Fuck no," Sophie breathes.

Chapter 3

Sophie is already out of bed when Cassia opens her eyes. She can hear her moving about in the kitchen. Probably cleaning up after last night's dinner. They hadn't wanted to clean up then, so eager were they to get to... *other* things. She smiles at the memory.

Morning sun streams in through the window slats, shining on her dark skin, piercing her eyes and breaking her reverie. She groans and rolls over, bringing the white blankets up over her unruly head of curls. After only about thirty seconds, though, she groans again, throws the blankets off, and rushes to the toilet. She saunters back, comfortable in her nudity for now, and begins making the bed. She carefully tucks each of the corners under the mattress as she hums a popular kantada to herself. When the sheets and blankets are all tucked in tight, she throws the pillows on haphazardly, in direct opposition to how carefully she'd made the bed. Both she and Sophie like being able to burrow in whenever the mood strikes them, and they've found it's easier to do so when the pillows are in a pile.

From the kitchen comes the sound of glass shattering, followed by, "Well, shit."

Cassia waits to hear if the broom closet door opens. When it doesn't, she sighs. She suspects Sophie is picking the glass up with her bare hands. She slips on well-loved house shoes and a fuzzy blue robe over her naked body, then pads out to the kitchen where Sophie is, indeed, picking up a shattered baking pan with bare hands. Cassia watches her for a minute, marveling that this beautiful, kind, and insufferable woman is hers.

"We have a broom, you know," Cassia says dryly, making her presence known.

Sophie looks up, shrugs, then continues to pick up glass. "Yes, but I'm in bare feet, and I'd have to walk through the broken glass to get to it."

"You could have called for me," Cassia walks to the broom closet and pulls the broom out.

"I thought it'd be nice if I could cook for you, for once. You always take such good care of me... Well, it seemed silly to wake you up when I wanted to surprise you...Ow!" She drops the glass shard she'd just picked up. The two of them watch numbly as pale blue blood, the blue of a frozen lake, drips slowly from her white finger.

"Sophie..." Cassia whispers. The broom clatters to the floor loudly. Neither of them notices. "Your blood..."

"Yes, I can see that. I... I guess I have it, then, don't I?" Sophie stumbles backward, out of the glass and into a convenient chair. "I guess that explains why I've been so cold despite the heat."

"You didn't tell me you've been cold." Cassia walks right through the glass, not caring whether her worn-thin rubber soles will protect her, and sits down next to her.

Sophie shrugs. "I didn't think I was sick, only... Well, you know me. I get weird flashes of hot and cold, always have. It's seemed worse lately but I didn't want to worry you."

"Too late now. I'm officially worried." She leans forward, elbows on her knees, and stares at Sophie.

"Well, what do we do now?" Sophie tremulously asks.

"The doctor should be in town today. We'll go see him, find out how far along you are. Maybe it's early enough it can be treated."

"Do you think?"

"I'm hoping, my love." She takes Sophie's hand in hers and squeezes absent-mindedly.

Chapter 4

Sophie is bundled up with gloves, long sleeves, and long pants. Her pale face pokes out from underneath a hand-knitted hat. Cassia, conversely, is dressed in light flowing pants and a short-sleeved top. They exit their home hand-in-hand and begin walking down Market Street. Both are quiet, lost in their own fears.

Cassia, tired of the quiet, asks, "Are you too warm?"

Sophie shrugs. "Not really. That's probably not a good sign, is it?"

Cassia shakes her head, going quiet again. The freezing disease, the newspapers christened it, because that's what it does to your blood over time. It's characterized by blue blood, even when oxidized, and increasingly cold blood temperatures, until the body begins shutting down – digestion, respiration, and finally heartrate. It's effectively hypothermia from the inside – a slow, torturous death, and only curable in the very early stages. So early that very few people notice soon enough, making the survival rate abysmally low. It's why the doctors recommend pricking oneself every week, but few people actually do it. Sophie included.

As they near the market, they encounter more people. Seeing Sophie bundled up, everyone gives them a wide berth. Faces that had just yesterday been full of welcome and excitement to see her are, today, closed and fearful. As far as anyone knows, it's not contagious, but that doesn't matter. Cassia moves closer to Sophie, a silent confirmation that she, at least, is not scared of her lover. Sophie reaches down and squeezes Cassia's hand. "It's okay, my love. I'm used to being the strange one, as the only American amongst Greeks."

"Yes, but that's different. Not that it matters. I would show my love and support for you regardless of the reason." Inwardly, she thinks of what she said to Anastasios the other day, about this being a community not just a town. Well, they're showing their true colors now.

They approach the doctor's tent quickly enough, though it feels like they've walked to the hangman's noose. It looks normal from the outside, with white curtains tied back. There are plants on either side of the entrance, large sages with delicate flowers. Cassia ushers Sophie inside, glad to be away from the eyes that were pretending not to stare. Through the window, she can see the asclepius next door, where she'd been praying just a few days ago. It's a purposeful juxtaposition; many find they wish to pray after visiting the doctor.

A large bronze bell rests on a counter, behind which a young woman with glasses sits chewing gum. After checking in with the receptionist, they sit down in the predictably uncomfortable brown chairs. There's bland art on the walls and even more bland music on the record player. Along the back wall is a line of curtains with a number above each one.

"Do you want me to go in with you?" Cassia asks.

"I'd like that. I hate doctors."

After about ten minutes the receptionist calls Sophie's name and the number three.

Cassia and Sophie stand up in unison, hands held tightly, and walk through the curtains. They step into another realm, a white room with sterile counters and stethoscopes and a tall man in a white lab coat. He turns to them, pulls a rope and the curtains fold down, encasing them from the outside world.

"Which one of you is the patient?" he asks, gruffly.

Sophie tentatively raises her right hand.

"Get undressed and into a hospital gown, then sit on the exam table." He turns around but does not leave. Not that there's anywhere for him to go.

Sophie slowly peels each layer off, eventually revealing her bare skin. Her veins seem more obvious than normal, but perhaps that's only because Cassia knows what they hold. Standing there naked, Cassia can see Sophie shivering from across the room. Sophie hurriedly dresses in the white and blue striped gown. Cassia thinks it makes her look even more frail. She vows in that moment that she'll do anything to help Sophie heal, that no prayer or sacrifice will be too much.

"Okay," Sophia says. "You can turn around now."

The doctor does. "So. What seems to be the problem?"

"I cut myself this morning and my blood... Well, it's blue."

"Do you prick yourself every week, as recommended?"

She shakes her head. "I know I should, I just... Well, I hate the sight of blood."

He sighs in exasperation. "When was the last time it was normal?"

"Um... maybe two months ago?"

"Well, let's see how progressed it is then." He starts pulling out phlebotomy equipment from a drawer – a syringe, tubes, the stretchy band to tie it off when he's done.

He ties the tourniquet around her upper right arm, then slides the syringe into a vein. Sophie lets out a tiny gasp at the prick. The doctor begins to draw. The blood that comes out is as blue as it was at their home. Cassia had been half hoping it was a fluke, that it had been in their heads or a trick of lighting. But no. Sophie is definitively sick.

When the doctor has drawn a full vial, he turns away, to where a microscope was hidden. He drops a couple beads of blood onto a petri dish and then inserts that into the microscope's tray. Cassia prays to Asclepius that it's in the early stages, that the medicine will still help; that there's hope.

The doctor laments and Cassia's hopes are dashed. She feels like that time she fell off the swing and had the wind knocked out of her.

"Well, you definitely have hemopágos. It looks like you might still be in the first stage, but you're rapidly approaching the second. The medicine may or may not help you; I recommend taking it either way. It won't hurt."

"Do you have any in stock?"

"No, you will have to go to the pharmako."

He takes out a pad from his pocket and begins writing. "Here. It's expensive but if we've caught it early enough, it will be worth it." He turns to Cassia. "And you. It's not contagious but even so, you should be testing yourself at least once a week. Don't take after her."

Cassia nods numbly. If Sophie can't be cured, Cassia knows she won't be able to keep up with the rigors of living.

"What if the medicine doesn't work? Is there anything else?"

"The Magi and prayers to Asclepius. And when those don't work, come back to me and I'll prescribe you pain medicine. They won't cure the disease, but they'll make the last days more bearable."

"What about... Well, do you know of anything from other pantheons?"

He shrugs. "I am not in the practice of studying other pantheons. You could try the American one."

Cassia snorts. "Their main God is not prone to saving people."

"Then you may as well stick with Asclepius."

They leave the clinic quietly, neither one knowing what to say. Cassia inclines her head to the temple questioningly, but Sophie shakes her head. They stop at the pharmako down the street. The medicine is indeed expensive but they are in a fortunate place that they can afford it. And like the doctor said, if it works, it will be worth it.

Cassia takes her hand and they begin to walk home, neither one hearing the vendors calling to the people around them. They are quiet as they walk, both of them stuck in their own heads and too stunned to speak. Reaching home, Sophie drops her jacket and they kick their shoes off in the entryway, not bothering to put any of it away. They walk up their stairs. Still without speaking, they both walk to their bedroom and sit down on their bed. Finally, Cassia clears her throat. "Well. What now?"

"Now I take the medicine. Maybe it'll work. Maybe it won't."

"And if it won't? Will you come pray to Asclepius with me?"

"Maybe I will come once." She shrugs. "But you know my opinion of the Gods."

"That they won't bother with petty humans like us? Even though we have been blessed twice by Hera and once by Aphrodite? Seems like they bother with us quite often." Cassia stands up and begins pacing.

"But maybe they shouldn't. Maybe human life is not something they should mess with. If the medicine doesn't work, then maybe it's my time to die."

"That's bullshit, Soph." She grabs a fistful of her long hair. "You're barely fifty-five. You still have a lot of life left in you."

Sophie sighs heavily. "Right now, I'm tired, Cass. Will you let me take a nap?"

"Of course, my love. Would you like me to make some fasolada for dinner?"

Sophie doesn't say anything, instead crawling into their bed. Her small form seems tiny all alone in the big bed.

"Would you like more blankets?" Cassia asks, wringing her hands.

"No." Sophie's voice is muffled in her cocoon of blankets and pillows, seemingly already mostly asleep.

Cassia goes into the study to begin her research.

Chapter 5

The next month passes by torturously. They fight often, talk less. The script stays the same – one woman begging the other to pray for absolution and healing, the other begging to be left alone. Neither one is able to see the other's point of view, nor wants to.

A week or so after taking the medicine, Sophie progresses from mere shivering. She gets slower and slower, both in her breathing and her movements. She gets clumsier, more irritable, and more forgetful. She wants to sleep all the time. In short, the medicine was too late. She does go to the asclepia once but it doesn't do anything. Cassia claims it is because Sophie didn't take it seriously. Sophie says it is because the Gods have already determined her fate.

They choose this time to tell Haris, once they know it is definite. He begins coming over to his mothers' house daily, bringing food, helping with dinner, and, most importantly, being a sounding board for both of them when they get fed up with each other.

After two weeks, Cassia is spending all her time at the bibliotheca, researching Gods of healing. All of them require the diseased person to be the one asking. Sophie's shivering increases and she is forbidden from holding anything glass, as she keeps on breaking things and they are running low on glassware.

After three weeks, Haris begins working with Cassia when she gets home from her research ventures. Sophie barely moves, preferring to sit with several blankets piled on next to the heater's output vent.

After four weeks, Haris and Cassia are still trying to find a Magi who can tell them something different, something none of the texts say – that it's possible to heal a patient from afar. Sophie's breathing is slowing down now, as is her pulse. They can all feel a point of no return coming. Cassia and Haris are getting desperate.

And so, today, Haris is busy trying to distract Sophie from the chill in her veins while Cassia goes on yet another research quest at the bibliotecha.

Which is fairly quiet, letting her spend the time re-reading the texts again and again without any interruptions, always hoping for a different answer. She sits in an overstuffed armchair by the window, the sun shining through quite lovely. Everything about this setup is, actually, quite lovely, except for the part about how she's researching ways to save her wife.

"There!" she whispers in triumph, her finger jabbing at a line. The title reads, "How Alcestis Sacrificed Herself to Save Her Husband." There must be something in this! She reads eagerly, mumbling pieces of the story. "Apollo was the slave... Gift that anyone could take his disease... Alcestis was the only one..." Her hopes are shattered before she reaches the end. She would have to sacrifice herself, if she could even procure such a boon. Well, she will keep that in reserve, should she need it.

She slams the book shut so hard that dust sloughs off it and hovers in the sun's rays. She stacks it on top of the pile of already perused books and turns to her pile of unread books. Which is empty. Well damn!

The only other occupant glares at her. She realizes she'd said that out loud, not in her head. She sighs and nods an apology. The young man, Nicholas from the butcher, looks away.

Cassia gets up and wanders the aisles, scanning the bookshelves and hoping to find a book she hasn't read yet. She doesn't find one. She growls at the shelves, knowing full well it won't do anything, but unable to help herself. She glances at the large clock overhanging the room. It's almost noon. Even though Sophie barely eats, her slowed digestion meaning she needs less, and Cassia barely eats because she can't stomach food knowing she has no way to keep Sophie alive, they still keep up with the habit of sitting down for a meal. She sighs and stomps up to the front.

On her way out she stops at the head librarian's desk. "Hey, Daphne."

The librarian looks up and smiles. "Hello, Cassia. I'm guessing you're here to ask me if any new books on healing have come in?"

"How'd you know?"

"That's the same question you've asked me every day this week. The answer is still no. I'll let you know tomorrow if it changes."

"Okay, thanks, Daphne."

Cassia walks through the market in a daze. She barely hears the vendors calling or notices the jostling people. That is, until she smells the honey wafting from the loukoumades booth. She smiles, thinking how much Sophie likes them and wouldn't it be nice to brighten her day a little bit? Even if Cassia failed to find what she was looking for, she can do this for Sophie. She has such a sweet tooth it'll be an easy way to get her to eat a little more than normal.

She gets in line, already excited at the prospect of seeing Sophie enjoy the little donuts. At first, she doesn't notice the conversation between the two gossiping old women in front of her, but then the word 'Magi' worms its way into her brain. She taps the smaller of the women on the shoulder. "What did you just say?"

"There's a visiting Magi in town. Some big shot, too. I've heard his tent is all the way in the center ring by the fire."

The other woman chimes in. "I've heard that too."

"Do you know what he specializes in?" Cassia can't keep the hope from seeping into her.

"Well, the Gods, of course. Isn't that what they all specialize in, in their own ways?" She titters.

The other woman leans in conspiratorially. "I heard he's actually spoken directly to the Gods."

She's barely able to contain her excitement. "Do you know what color tent he has?"

"Blue with purple trim."

She stays in line long enough to get the donuts only because she knows how happy they'll make Sophie. She feels like she's vibrating by the time she gets to the front of the line

She practically runs home, brimming with hope and two dozen honey donuts. When she gets home, she takes a few moments downstairs to catch her breath, not wanting to alarm Sophie. Composed, she walks upstairs to find her wife and son in the living room next to the heating vent. She sits down next to Sophie and wraps her in a tight hug.

"You seem happy," Sophie comments.

"I'm just happy to be home, really. I got your favorite, loukoumades. Fresh from the bakery down the street. They're in the kitchen."

"Would you bring them in here? I am quite comfortable."

"Of course, my love." Cassia gets up and walks into the kitchen, retrieving the bag of donuts. She'll talk to Haris after Sophie goes to sleep.

She sits back down with the bag and the three of them share the perfectly crispy confections, licking the honey off their fingers after each one. For once, there is no food left when they're done.

Chapter 6

The air is cold and clear in the predawn as Cassia slinks out of the house. The stars show fiercely even as a pale sliver of light creeps from the east. As it grows, bringing the promise of warmth to the city, a mist forms, progressing into a dense fog. Thick and heavy, it settles so that where once the clarity of a bitter night reigned, now Cassia can barely see the leaves of the trees that hang over Market Street. The mist drips upon the dry leaves gathered in piles along the edges of the street. One could hardly be faulted for not seeing her dark figure as she slithers along the building line. She is clad in a long green cloak that obscures all but the black of her boots, her arms folded into the heavy cloth, hood drawn up over her head, hiding her face lest Sophie happens to peer out of the window. She does not. Cassia's gaze fixes once more upon the road before her, brown eyes piercing through the fog and dark. She starts walking away from the market, towards the Magi.

She walks more naturally once she's out of sight of the house. Sophie probably knows she's going – there have been enough disagreements that she must know Cassia wants to do something more – but even so, Cassia doesn't want yet another fight.

Cassia sighs, remembering the deep blue veins so apparent on Sophie's white body last night, a vicious map of the disease's progress.

She wraps her cloak tighter around her to fight the thickening fog. Or perhaps she's cold because she's thinking about Sophie. They've been keeping the house warmer than normal, in an attempt to give her more freedom of movement and not simply lay in bed under a mountain of blankets. It isn't working.

At least Haris is taking the news well. Or, as well as a young college student can take the news that his mom is dying.

A few blocks ahead, just past the ruins, are the Magi's current quarters. They live in tents and are semi-nomadic. They move around the town's boundaries, sometimes up Mount Olympos to gain greater access to the Gods' wisdom, but are always within a day's travel of Dion.

She enters the camp and makes her way through the maze-like layout, searching for the blue tent with purple trim, the one closest to the fire. The color and placement are both a sign of his esteem and power. She vibrates with hope and excitement that this Magi will know a way.

She finds the tent without trouble and rings the bell hanging from the pole outside it.

"Enter," a wizened voice calls out.

She pulls back the tent flap and walks in, finding a smoky room with ample cushions surrounding a central fire. The walls are stone, the floor also stone but covered with a plush Persian rug. There is a table piled high with books and scrolls. And there, in the center by the fire, is a thin, bald, mostly naked, and very wrinkly man smoking a pipe. She's impressed – this is the most elaborate and magical Magi tent she's seen.

She coughs from the heavy smoke, then bows deeply to the ancient man.

"Be at ease, child. What brings you to me?" he asks, his voice even more gravelly up close.

"I seek a way to petition the Gods directly. Do you know of a way? Or of a way to heal someone without them asking?"

"What will you pay me for this knowledge?"

She purses her lips. "What do people normally pay for such knowledge?"

"I'd take fifty drachma."

She starts in surprise. "I was expecting something magical."

He shrugs. "I need dinner tonight. You don't think the Gods provide parchments and food, do you?"

"I didn't think about it like that. Well, here." She hands over the money. "I hope you enjoy dinner."

He takes a deep draw from his pipe, then nods. "Now back to your question. It is not easy. You will need to sacrifice three animals at three different locations along the map, at which point the portal should open and you can petition the Gods. Do you have a map of Mount Olympos?"

Cassia shakes her head. "No, I didn't think of it."

He harumphs, then calls out loudly. "Georges!"

"Yeah?" A second man returns the yell.

"You still have that map of Mount Olympos?"

"I think so. Let me check." They hear crashing and banging as he apparently rearranges a music shop, looking for said map. "Found it!" he shouts in triumph. He sounds so excited Cassia can almost believe he has a personal stake in the outcome.

A large, round man wearing bright red pants and a pirate shirt appears in the entryway, proudly holding the map aloft.

"Bring it," commands the Magi, and he does.

The ancient man gets up and spreads the map across the table, pushing the books and scrolls aside. He draws a lopsided star at the base of the mountain. "You will need to sacrifice an animal here, and say an incantation."

She begins to speak, but he cuts her off.

"I'll provide you exactly what to say at each location." He then draws another star halfway up the mountain. "You will then need to sacrifice an animal here, and say the second incantation." He finally draws a third star on the summit, the peak of Mytikas. "And here, again, an animal sacrifice, an incantation, and some herbs. The herbs will be crucial to determining which God you get; I will provide you lists of that, as well. Can you do that?" He scans her body, looking for health and strength.

"I've climbed to Skala Peak before. I'm sure that, for Sophie, I can make it to Mytikas."

"Hm. How long ago?" He looks doubtful.

She shrugs. "A couple years maybe. It hasn't been long. I think I still have the strength and stamina."

"Hmph. You will not get a second chance, I imagine."

"No, this is it. I'm out of chances. Can I take the tram? Can I bring anyone with me? Tell me what the specifics are."

"No tram and no one else; it must cost you something. The animals you can sacrifice are female goats or chamois, chickens, and other birds. And here are the incantations." He grabs a sheaf of papyrus and starts copying down, in beautiful script, the words she'll need to say. "Study these and memorize them. You don't want to read from the papyrus; you will need to have them memorized or it won't work as well."

She nods vigorously. "I can do that."

"Good. Then here are the herbs you'll need, depending on which God you desire." He hands her another sheet. "Don't get it wrong or you might get Zeus. He's known for being capricious at best, cruel at worst."

"Okay, thank you. You have no idea how grateful I am."

He shrugs. "Well, I hope for your sake, and your wife's."

She carefully places the precious papers into her satchel, then secures it with its clasp. She tucks it against her side, then nods to the Magi. Stepping out of the tent, the bright sunlight stuns her. It had been dark when she'd entered and now... She checks her time piece. And now it's mid-morning. Haris will surely have told on her by now, which means Sophie will likely be furious again. As she walks home, she belatedly realizes she never told him Sophie was her wife.

When Cassia returns home, she walks in to find Sophie waiting for her at the kitchen table, a mug of something hot in her hands. She's still dressed in her pajamas and her hair is a tangled mess. Haris sits next to her, dressed in a sleeveless white peplos, a glass of lemonade with ice cubes in front of him.

"Oh. Hi," she says, inanely trying to hide the papyrus behind her back.

"Hi, Cassia. I know where you went. Haris blabbed."

"Sorry." Haris shrugs, then leans in to Sophie. "Mom, I need to go do some studying. I'll see you tomorrow, okay?"

"Alright, dear. Take the tram home, will you? I hate to think of you walking through some of those neighborhoods by yourself."

Haris nods. "Okay, Mom. I love you both." He grabs his pack and heads for the door.

Cassia chimes in, "It was good to see you, Haris." He has been here more often these past few weeks, some nights even camping out on the couch. But even so, seeing him is one of the small joys she still has in her days.

After Haris leaves, Cassia and Sophie sit in uncomfortable silence for several minutes. Finally, Sophie breaks the silence. "So, I guess you could tell me what you found out today. I can see the excitement wafting off you."

"Oh. Well then. In good news, I may have found the answer..."

"The answer I didn't want you to find?"

"Yes! No! I don't know. It's the answer where you don't die but also don't have to go against your own beliefs. The one where..."

"Where you save me. Like I'm some damsel in distress. I'm not, you know. Damsels in distress usually want to be saved. Hence the distress. I may be a damsel but I'm not in distress, Cassia, and I wish you wouldn't act like it."

"I'm sorry, Soph, but you're dying! That's distressing! And you refuse to try not to die, which is even more distressing. After all the Gods have done for us, I just don't get why you won't take this extra step now to save yourself."

"Those other times… It was about life. It was about living our lives, about getting married and about having a baby. This is death, Cass, and I just… I don't think the Gods should mess with that."

"No, it's about the continuation of your life. About you being around for our son, and his life."

"You can twist it all you want; I still won't agree with you."

"That's fine, you don't have to. I'm still going to do everything I can to save your life."

"You're trying to make up for not being able to save your parents."

"No!" She purses her lips. "Maybe. But it's not just that, Soph. They died in a freak accident and I couldn't save them, and then I was alone for so long. When I found you, I finally felt like I wasn't alone anymore."

"So, you don't want to be alone."

"NO! Now you're twisting my words. I want to be with **you**. And yeah, I don't want to lose you like I lost my parents, but it's not just about being alone, it's about you're my person. My only person."

"I'm too tired to keep fighting with you, Cass." She gets up slowly.

Cassia takes her hand. "Please, Sophie. Try thinking about what you'd do if it was me instead. Wouldn't you try everything to help me?"

"I wouldn't have to. You'd do it all yourself." She tugs her hand free and gingerly walks toward the bedroom.

Cassia follows. "Can I… Can I make you some food?"

Sophie leans against the door frame. "Some soup would be helpful. Or a sandwich. Or both. I'm actually starving."

"Coming right up. Why don't you cocoon yourself and I'll bring lunch in when it's ready." She chokes out the words. This sudden increase in hunger is an expected but also bad sign, per the doctor. It means her body needs more fuel to keep going. As disturbing as her previous lack of hunger was, this sudden voracity is even more so.

Sophie nods, then makes her way to the bed, where she buries herself under blankets.

After Sophie is done eating and falls asleep, Cassia sits at the kitchen table, head in her hands and staring blankly at the table. She remembers purchasing this table with Sophie, twenty-some years ago. They'd picked it out for its solidity. The top is a huge slab of wood, each leg like a tree trunk, all polished to a mirror shine. It's held up well, given all the school projects and family dinners and game nights they'd had on it. She slides a palm over the top. They've never had to get it repolished, in all these years. Will this table really outlast Sophie, she wonders.

"By the Gods, I will not let that happen," she says to the empty room.

Then, Cassia pulls out a map of Greece and lays it out across the family table. She begins mapping out the way from Dion to Litochoro, and from Litochoro to Mount Olympos. It's been decades now since she climbed it – since she used to go with her father. She's determined not to let that stop her. She grabs a pencil and begins tracing the map onto a spare sheet, so she has one to bring with her. She traces small but carefully; she doesn't want to make any mistakes that could cause her to get lost but also wants to take up less paper. The less paper, the less likelihood of losing something.

When her mapping is done, she pulls out the incantations and sheets of materials needed. She takes note of the materials she'll need to pick up – she'll do that tomorrow, she plans. Then rewrites each incantation separately, with the materials needed for each. Finally, all writing done, she begins to memorize them, as instructed. She won't get anything wrong.

Chapter 7

A couple of days later, after Cassia single-mindedly memorized all the incantations and her route to Mount Olympos, she is ready. She is dressed in thick woolen pants over a thin layer of linen, as well as a wool shirt. She is packing a backpack while Sophie glares at her from the door jamb. She has before her two pairs of clothes, a bedroll, two blankets, a selection of dried foods, and an insulated bag for some foods that need to be kept cool. When Sophie finally speaks, her voice is as tired as she looks.

"You can't do this. You're too old, Cassia, and so am I. My time is up."

Cassia stops packing and throws her hands up. She's had this fight so many times already and is tired of it. "I don't care how old either of us is! I'm not going to sit around and watch you freeze to death, not when it's possible to do something!"

Sophie walks like her bones are made of glass over to Cassia and rests her hand on Cassia's back. "We all must die eventually, my love." She then sits down on the edge of the bed.

"Yes, eventually!" She pinches the bridge of her nose. "You're too young to die. We're only in our fifties, Soph. I'm going to do something to save you, even if you don't want me to."

"I want my last days to be **with** you. Please, my love, don't leave me now." Sophie holds a sob back, swallowing thickly.

"I have to. I can't live knowing I could have done something but didn't." Cassia continues packing but haphazardly, throwing things in rather than folding them.

"The Gods may not even listen! We've already been lucky three times. The odds that they'll listen yet again are slim."

"Or perhaps they're high." When her pack won't close, she takes everything out and proceeds with more care this time. She speaks quietly now, almost too quietly to be heard. "Tell me truly. You have been beating around the bush all this time. Why are you so insistent that you have to die?"

"Because there is always a price to these things." She fidgets with the scar from her missing pinky on her left hand, then looks over at a picture of Haris on the wall. Cassia follows her gaze. "And I'm scared it will be a price I am not willing to pay."

"Oh, Soph. They wouldn't exact that price. That would be too high even for them."

"You don't know that, Cassia. Please, don't go. Just stay. For once, listen to me."

"What are you talking about? I listen to you all the time!" Her pack won't close yet again and she throws it across the room. It hits the wall and the overflowing items spill out onto the floor.

"Well, no, not all the time. You don't listen to me about putting the dishes in the washer instead of the sink, or separating your whites from your colors, or about not walking by yourself in the pre-dawn mornings!" The volume of Sophie's voice rises with each word until she's yelling and out of breath at the end.

"Those are... I listen to you about the important stuff."

"Not getting mugged is important!"

"You know what I mean. I listen to you about how you feel, the way you think about politics and the world and..."

Sophie smiles ruefully. "None of it matters anyway, Cassia. I want you with me in my last days. And I don't want to pay the price for me to live. Please."

"And I don't want to see your last days happen yet! I refuse to accept that you have to die. And I refuse to believe the cost will be too high. I won't let it be." Cassia's shoulders drop. "It'll only take me... Six days, max. If it doesn't work, I'll come back. I'll be here for the end. I will."

Sophie shakes her head. "You don't know how much longer I have, though. It could be days or it could be two weeks. I might be dead already when you return."

"Then let us not part with a fight. Please, Sophie, know that I have to do this, and try to hold on until I return."

Sophie finally gives up. She gets up and gets Cassia's pack, then sits back down and calmly begins packing it, rolling the clothes tightly, squeezing the last bits of air out of the food bags, and finally securing the bedroll to the outside of the pack. It closes. "I will try my best, Cassia, but it might be out of my control. Just... Be careful. There are dangers on the mountain."

"I know. I will come back to you, I vow it."

"I believe you. I still don't want you to go, but I believe you will come back. I hope it's in time."

Cassia picks her pack up, then cradles Sophie's face in two hands. "I love you. Hold out for me. I will make you a miracle."

Sophie nods, unable to hold back her tears any longer, and pushes Cassia away. "Then go, if you must."

Cassia nods once, kisses Sophie deeply, and then walks into the kitchen. Sophie follows her. They walk downstairs. Cassia pulls her fur jacket out of the closet and puts it on, then shoulders her pack. She almost takes out a bow and quiver from the closet, but then leans it back up against the wall. Sophie has packed her enough food to last her a year. She does, however, take a hatchet out of the closet and straps it to her pack. Finally, she's ready. On opening the front door, they find Haris about to knock.

"Hi," he says. "Are you really going?"

"Yes," Cassia answers. "Do you disagree?"

He shakes his head. "If anything can save her, I'm all for it. I want my mom to live for a long time yet. Just be safe, Mitéra."

Cassia hugs Haris. "I will. Take care of her for me, okay? Make sure she stays warm, and that she eats. I will be back before the end either way."

Cassia steps out the front door, then turns around for one last look at the two people she loves most. Haris appears to be holding Sophie upright. Tears stream down her face. Cassia hopes she won't regret leaving.

Chapter 8

The first thing she sees on walking out the front door is Mount Olympos in the far distance, blue with a small cap of white at the top. There will be a small amount of snow already, then. She's glad for the boots and thick jacket, though she might wish for more before the trip is done.

Walking away from the home she created with Sophie is hard. Not harder than she expected, as she knew it would be possibly the hardest thing she's ever done. But the aftermath is unexpected: the constant worry over Sophie's health, whether Haris is taking care of her, whether she's letting him. Whether Cassia will, indeed, succeed or fail. All of this feels like a dark, heavy cloud following her, trying to suffocate her. She breathes heavily, and turns down the road away from the market. She'll pass the Magi's tents on her way out, but won't stop there. She's gotten all she can out of them.

The walk isn't hard. She's always been a heavy walker, choosing her feet over trams or carriages. Daily walks to the market and a healthy diet have kept her fairly fit, even into her fifties. Though she suspects the last leg of the hike up the mountain will give her some trouble. She should pick up some rope in Litochoro; that might come in handy.

The paved road turns into hard-packed dirt from all the travelers to and from Mount Olympos or Litochoro. Though some hike up the mountain from here, to reach the highest summit one has to go into the other town. So many seeking miracles just like her from the Greek Gods. She wonders how many have gotten the miracles they sought, and how many had to walk home no better off than before.

"Please," she whispers. "Let me save Sophie."

She turns a bend and comes upon an old man sitting by the side of the path, wearing only a loincloth and holding out an empty bowl. She fishes in her pocket and hands over a drachma. He bites into it, as though to verify it's real, and then nods his thanks. She nods back.

Before she can continue on her way, though, she hears the shuffling of feet. She turns to find a tall man garbed in the rainbow of colors coming up behind her. He drops in his own drachma and comments, "It's always good to help the poor. Never know when the Gods may be testing us."

She shakes her head and speaks with passion, surprising herself. "I don't do it for fear of the Gods. They have no need of silver. I do it because if the poor aren't Gods, then they actually need the silver."

"You feel very strongly about this," he mutters.

"I do!" She even stomps her foot. "There are so many people that do good when they think the Gods might be watching, but turn nasty any time they think they can get away with it. And these people, who are vile at heart, live long, full lives, while my wife, who is truly good and kind, gets sick and is dying."

"That doesn't seem fair," he placates. "I should be going now."

"Yeah, suppose so..." She trails off, realizing she was taking her anger out on a stranger. It's not his fault; he might not be one of those people she resents so strongly. He might actually be a decent person who also does things a certain way when the Gods might be watching.

She begins walking again.

She walks for two boring hours on dusty paths, the only human interaction coming from the occasional beggar who's set up on side of the road. She'd brought extra drachma to give out, but unfortunately, by about three-quarters of the way, her spare purse has run out. While her generosity is large, she also knows she must take care of herself enough to save Sophie and doesn't dip into her main purse, even though she wants to.

She crests a small hill and looks out across to Litochoro, nestled at the base of the mountain, red-tiled buildings peeking out from between the green forest. The mountain sits behind the city like a watchful mother. The city is bustling, people moving about their days visible even from the distance. She'll stop for lunch, then begin her trek up the mountain to the first sacrifice site. She doesn't have much farther to go today, only to the first site. Tomorrow she'll reach the second, then make her way almost to the top. The third sacrifice has to be at dawn so she'll camp out just below the summit. The way down will be easier as she'll be able to take her time — if she's not in a hurry to get home, that is.

She weaves through town, finding her way to the market by following the flow of people. Those empty-handed are heading there, for the most part, and those with bags of food are leaving. She makes it finally, and that's good, for she is starving.

A belltower overshadows the market, its bell tolling to mark it as exactly noon. Her stomach growls almost on cue; she and Sophie almost always have lunch at this time. She begins to scout for food, planning to save what she packed for the trek up the mountain where there won't be food stalls. Here will be her last good meal for at least three days, so she intends to eat well. She opts for two lamb gyros and sits down at a nearby bench. The pita is soft and pillowy, the meat flavorful and tender, the perfect mix of spices. She moans quietly. The cool tzatziki sauce drips down her chin and into her shirt, all the way between her breasts. Nervously, she checks if anyone is watching her, and when everyone seems engrossed in their own personal dramas, discreetly cleans up after herself. She eats the rest of the gyros more carefully, not wanting to lose any more tzatziki or to mess up her clothes. She has a long time to be in them.

She stands up, throws her trash away, then picks up her pack and begins winding through the market. Vendors call to her, and she experiences a brief moment of nostalgia, thinking back to that day before they found out. How simple things were then, how straightforward. And now, everything is a toss-up, whether she'll succeed, whether she'll make it back in time. For all she knows, Sophie could already be dead and this will be for naught. But no, if that's the case, she'll go to the underworld and petition Hades himself if she has to. But unlike Orpheus, she will succeed. It doesn't matter what she has to do, if only Sophie can stay with her a little bit longer.

So caught up in her imaginings, she doesn't even notice that she has passed through the rest of the town and finds herself walking up toward Mount Olympos. "Shit," she groans. "I forgot to buy the sacrificial animals! What should I buy? Chickens? Goats? A cage of chickens would probably be the easiest to carry."

"Ahem," a voice says behind her. "Can you talk to yourself a bit more out of the way?"

"Hm?" She turns around to find a tiny old woman, a scarf on her head and a basket of vegetables in her hand, glaring at her. "Oh. Sorry, yes, I'll be going now."

She turns back around, weaving between people and buildings to get back to the market. She's going in the opposite direction of most people now, as the market is almost closed, and she has to fight the current. It takes her longer to get back to the market than it did to leave.

Once there, she scans quickly, then spots the chicken vendor already packing up next to the central fountain. A light mist sprays her when she nears, and she shies away, not wanting her clothes to get wet. "Excuse me? I know you're packing up, but could I still purchase three chickens?"

The stooped man turns around, his face covered in wiry white hair. "Sorry, miss. All out. You can come back tomorrow, though. The market runs from 7 am to 2 pm."

Her shoulders sag. "That—that's too late."

She turns and finds all the vendors packing up. She is about to give up when she sees one vendor still with an animal: a single beautiful white goat. She walks over in a rush, needing to get there before anyone else. "I'll take it. And any other animals you might have."

The woman shrugs. "It's just her, now. 100 drachma."

"Here," Cassia says, handing over all but one of her remaining drachma. In return, she is handed the goat's leash. She tugs. The goat stares at her. She tugs again. He stares harder. Helplessly, she looks to the vendor.

"She only moves for food."

"Oh. Well, do you happen to have food she likes?"

"It'll be one drachma."

Chapter 9

As she leaves town again, she stays more observant this time, noting the stonework of the houses she passes and the beautiful gardens. Litochoro was one of the places she and Sophie had considered living, but feared it would be too touristy. They'd liked Dion for its proximity to the mountain while being far enough away that it wouldn't be overrun with people come the sacrificial season.

Cassia reaches the trail head and can move no farther. Literally. She turns and sees the goat staring at her again. She waves a piece of dried fruit, and the goat takes a step. Cassia sighs. Is this animal really going to do this the whole way? She moves the morsel slowly away, and the goat follows. So, she walks backward up the trail, seeing the massive platane trees from above rather than below. Their pale bark looks like tombstones. She shakes the image off and focuses instead on her feet. The ground is covered with their shed leaves. She sighs in awe; many of these trees are probably hundreds of years old. This forest will survive long after her; they care little for her drama.

Every hundred feet or so the goat gets the better of her, and gets the food before she can pull it out of reach. Luckily, she has a good-sized bag of it. The goat just needs to live long enough to be sacrificed.

She moves up toward the mountain with a handful of other people, all of them sickly, some of them with their own animals to sacrifice. Wanting to make it to the first site before night, she pushes herself past them as gently as she can manage, avoiding wheelchairs and canes. She wonders how far some of these people intend to make it, and whether they've already tried other, easier to access, temples. They probably have; a pilgrimage to Mount Olympos is usually the last resort.

Cassia stops at a waterfall, then squats to fill up her water skein. It takes a bit of maneuvering, to fill up her skein while still holding onto the goat's leash. Once full, she sits for a few extra minutes, enjoying the simple beauty of water falling over rocks. There's something calming about the knowledge that these rocks are slowly being ground down by the water. They too will outlast her lifetime, of course, but there's something reassuring about the fact that even rocks change over time.

She begins walking again. The trail is surrounded by a thick forest of pine, fir and birch trees. She hears bird calls and squirrels chirruping. The tree cover provides a nice level of shade, compared to the trek to town. Even though she's not pleased with the reason for being here, it's still a healing space and she feels peaceful here. She feels hopeful, even, that this will all work out for the best.

After a couple hours of moderate hiking, she makes it to the first sacrifice site. It's blissfully empty. She walks up to the altar, dragging the goat. She has just one piece of food left. She places it on top of the altar and then raises her eyebrows at the goat, who sits down.

Dropping her pack and rolling up her sleeves, she watches the goat from the corner of her eye as she pulls out the herbs for this sacrifice – Bay leaf for divining the will of the Gods, Milkweed for Asclepius, and Sage for healing to indicate her need. Then, a butcher's knife, picked up from Nicholas at the butcher's and then blessed by the Magi.

She lifts the goat onto the altar with much bleating and kicking. After a brief struggle, she manages to slit the sacrifice's throat; she gets kicked in the shoulder by a stray hoof but is able to keep the blood off her clothes. She looks down at the altar again. When the blood pools, she drops the herbs into the blood one by one. She recites the incantation.

"I call upon thee, Asclepius, at this first altar.
I call upon thee, Asclepius, to consider me worthy of an audience.
I give you Milkweed, your namesake,
And Bay leaf to divine your will,
And Sage for its healing properties,
Doused in the blood of this fine goat."

The blood boils and steams, running in rivulets across the altar top. After a couple of minutes, it cools down and coagulates. This is what the Magi told her would happen, that the blood would boil but she shouldn't expect anything at the first altar. Or the second. But by the third, the Gods should hear her. Or so she's been promised.

Cassia wipes the knife and her sticky hands clean on some leaves from the ground and walks away from the altar, massaging her shoulder as she does. It's not broken, but it will bruise. She leaves the carcass of the goat for the animals to eat. The Magi said she shouldn't eat the meat, as it has to be a sacrifice on her part. Not that the Gods want it anymore; it's served that purpose.

She begins her ascent again, a little lighter without the goat but still feeling it in the muscles of her thighs. She's not young anymore, and she will definitely feel her age tonight. But she wants to make sure she reaches at least halfway before stopping, so she only has the other half tomorrow. She plans to camp below the snow line, but close enough that she can make it to the summit by sunrise.

A group of four hikers pass her by. They're all in their twenties, she guesses, and this is probably an easy hike for them.

"You all right, Grandma?" one of them asks her in an American accent, turning around to look as he walks away.

She wheezes just a tiny amount as she attempts to talk and hike simultaneously. "Fine. And I'm a not a grandma yet."

He laughs. "My bad! No offense, yo." He turns back around and catches up to his friends.

Now she laments her age. Soph would surely tell her 'I told you so.' But that's okay. She'll make it; it will just take her longer than them. Twenty years ago, she might even have made it up and down again all in one day. That's not the case anymore, and she hopes only that Sophie can wait for her to make the trek. The Magi had said it must be a sacrifice and this surely will be, but she hopes Sophie's life isn't part of that.

She finally makes it to the halfway point, the refuge. She stops in to see if they have any rooms but, as she expected, they're all booked up. This is why she brought a bedroll and blankets, anyway. She scans the predesignated camping sites for a flat one. There's no fire ring, so she uses stones to create one. Next, she harvests small sticks for kindling, surrounding pine needles with the sticks, then larger sticks for the top of the fire. Eventually she unhooks her hatchet and proceeds to chop some larger branches and ta da! She has warmth for the night.

The fire built and lit, the pine wood burns a little smoky but with a pleasant aroma. Cassia pulls out her dinner – dried jerky and nuts, a definite step down from the delicious gyros in Litochoro. Still, the simple fare replenishes her stomach from the day's hike and she sighs as she eats, satisfied.

She retrieves her biography of the Gods, The Palace of Olympos, and flips through the pages. She's hoping she'll summon Asclepius, that she'll be brought straight to his quarters since he doesn't have a spot in the throne room. But in case she doesn't, she wants to get their names right so as not to offend a God or Goddess.

She scans each page for the relevant symbology and style of dress, as well as each God or Goddess' preferred moniker. Zeus sits on the center throne, which holds an eagle on its arm. The eagle is golden with ruby eyes. That should be recognizable. Who else? Hera usually appears as a stately, matronly figure, upright or enthroned with a polos crown, and her throne is ivory with three crystal steps leading up to it, with golden cuckoos and willow leaves decorating the back. Those are the two most important to remember, she supposes. The two most likely to smite her if she calls them the wrong names. She continues reading anyway, just in case. The more she knows, the more likely she'll be successful.

Chapter 10

Sophie sits at the bay window off the kitchen. It's one of the things she used to love about their home, this big window and that it was so close to downtown. She used to like watching people outside go about their daily lives. So full of life and purpose. But now it reminds her of that day not so long ago when Cassia came home to find her and Haris talking, when the biggest tragedy then was the state of Haris's love life. And now, only a month and some days later, so much has changed. The tragedy is her, now. A sludge-like tear meanders down her cheek. She wipes it away in frustration – even her tears are getting icier. She stands up slowly and creeps into the kitchen to heat some more tea. She miscalculates and crashes her hip into the kitchen table on her way. She begins to cry in earnest, even despite the slushiness of her tears.

Haris comes running up the steps, a paper bag in his hand. He throws it down on the table and two bottles of pills fall out. Her name, Sophie Vasiliadas, is written on the side, followed by Oxycodone. Gently he takes her by the shoulders, looking into her eyes. "Mom! What happened?"

Sophie shrugs. "I ran into the table. It's not a big deal, really..."

Haris lets go of her and steps back. "Let me see."

Sophie lifts her shirt up and her pants down just enough to show her hip bone. A deep blue bruise is already forming, but the skin did not break.

"It's not cut, Mom."

She nods. "I know. I don't know why I'm still crying. The pain isn't even that bad."

"You miss her."

Sophie nods, continuing to cry icy tears. "Oh, fuck, Haris, I do, I miss your mitéra. I wish she hadn't gone."

"I wish no such thing. I'm glad she went, Mom. If there's anything that can be done, we need to do it. We both need you."

"Oh, you don't need me. I'm a mess all the time."

"We love you anyway."

"I love you too. Both of you. But I don't think there's anything else to do but let me die."

"Mitéra and I are banking on a different answer. But she'd better hurry. I don't know..."

"How much longer I have? Yeah, it seems to be getting worse quickly."

He suddenly grabs her in a tight hug. "Let me make you some warm soup and get you under the covers. The doctor did say keeping you warm might slow it down, didn't he?"

"He said it might. But no guarantees; every patient is different."

"Well, let's do everything we can to hold out for Mitéra. I got you the pain meds, too."

Together they walk into the bedroom and he proceeds to layer blanket after blanket upon her, until there's a mountain of warmth upon her tiny figure.

Sophie shakes her head. "I don't want to take those unless I have to."

"Because they're addictive? You do hope to outlast this disease!"

"I'm not putting anything past your mitéra. If I have to survive this, I don't want to come out the other side with a vicious addiction."

He smiles. "I'm going to go set up the couch. I'm staying here until Mitéra comes home." He walks out of the room and she can hear him moving about the living room.

When he leaves, Sophie wishes he'd stay away. It'd almost be easier to be sick alone than with your child around. She still feels like she needs to take care of him, which leaves her nothing left to take care of herself. She lays there, buried under the blankets, but her self-pity is even heavier. She doesn't care so much that she's dying, only that she's doing it without the love of her life and having to take care of her son while she does it.

Chapter 11

Cassia wakes up when the cold seeps through her blankets. It's still dark out – the stars above shine brightly, Cassiopeia and Andromeda and more watching her. There's no hint of the sun coming up. She tries tugging the blankets tighter, hoping that will let her get another hour or so of sleep, but she starts shivering. Well, that answers that. She might as well get up and make breakfast. Starting a morning fire will help warm her up at least.

She preps the fire – luckily there is wood left over from last night, so she doesn't have to forage in the dark – then lights it. After a few minutes, the wood is caught. Filling up her kettle with water, she sets it down next to the fire, handle facing outward. When it heats up, she uses a thick stick to fish it away from the fire. A couple minutes is all it takes for the handle to cool. She pours water followed by tea leaves into a mug, then wets a hand towel. She wipes her face down with the warm, wet towel and sighs. It's not a warm shower, but it feels pretty dang good all the same.

She falls into a trance, remembering camping with her father. Her mother always stayed home because she didn't care for outdoor activities.

"You should know the old ways, kiddo. How to fend for yourself, how to take care of yourself."

Her father stands above her while she watches him with adoring eyes. Her father on one knee showing Cassia how to skin a rabbit. How to hold a knife. How to wield a bow without clipping one's own cheek. How to start a fire. With each image Cassia is a little bit taller, slowly growing into herself, and her father is a little bit more hunched.

They used to go out every month in the warm months. But it's been years, many long years, since she last went out with him – years even before his death. It's a wonder she remembers as much as she does – a testament, perhaps, to the sheer number of times they did camp.

She remembers her bow, sitting back at home. He had made it for her sixteenth birthday, just prior to their last camping trip. She wasn't good at it, and didn't give herself the time to become good. After that she became too cool to go camping with her dad, and he died before she could get over that teenage foolishness. She sets the long-held sorrow aside when her stomach rumbles.

Fishing out the sausage from the cold bag she packed, she sticks two on a long, thin stick and slowly roasts them. They've already been cooked through and could be eaten cold, but she feels the warm food will warm up her insides better and she'll feel better prepared for the hike ahead of her. The incline is only going to get steeper from here.

Sipping at her tea, the sharp tang of the tannins helps wake her up further. She takes a bite of sausage, which drips juice onto her fingers. She wipes them on her pants then takes another sip of tea. "Hm." She thinks about Sophie – when is she not, of course, but drinking tea reminds her of all the times they've drunk tea together.

The two of them sit in a Japanese garden, sipping tea and laughing.

They sit in their dining room, at their sturdy wooden table, holding hands and blowing on hot tea.

Sitting together at night, one arm wrapped around each other's waist, tea mugs in each spare hand.

Empty tea mugs on the table while they help Haris with homework.

Sophie shows Cassia a coffee machine in the market that she wants. "But you're the only one who drinks coffee!" Cassia protests.

Cassia setting up the coffee machine in the kitchen.

Now she wishes she had a crystal ball, to peer into their home and see Sophie. What is she doing? How is she doing? Cassia imagines her asleep in the large bed all by herself, wrapped up like a mummy. She imagines her fumbling through the house, struggling to make herself food. Is Haris helping to take care of her? Cassia hopes so.

The sky is lightening, finally, and she expects to see the sun soon. That will also warm her up. She stretches, cat-like, then begins packing up. If the sun is going to rise, it'd be good to get back on the trail with it. She'll avoid other people that way, hopefully, and get done with her task for the day sooner. She doesn't care for sacrificing animals. It feels wasteful, to leave all that meat. But it must be done, if she wants to succeed.

Her pack ready, she puts it on, then uses the last of the kettle water to douse the fire. Steam billows up and spirals into the sky. She watches it for a minute, transfixed. Sunlight peeks over the summit and light particles dance in the smoke. She comes back to herself at the sight of the sun, and she scuffs dirt over the remnants of her fire just in case. She doesn't want to cause a forest fire today.

She begins to hike and almost instantly her right leg gives out on her, excruciating pain shooting up and down its length. She gasps from the pain and instinctively puts her hand out to catch herself on a birch tree near her. She uses its stability to prop herself up, resting her head on the bark. She feels queasy and wonders whether she'll actually throw up.

"Well, this is just lovely," she mutters.

She hears laughter, and looks over to the refuge. A group of twenty-somethings comes barreling out. Lo and behold it's the same group as yesterday, the four young men who'd called her a grandma. They see her now and approach.

"Hey," the same kid as before says. He has sandy blonde hair and his cheeks are round. His baby face currently reads concern. "You don't look so hot."

"I seem to have a cramp in my leg. I don't think I pulled anything." She's sweating now, despite the cold, and she wipes a hand over her face to try and dry it.

"Maybe you should rest for the day?" the kid suggests.

"No, I need to do this today. It's... Well, my wife is dying. I need to get to the top before she dies."

"Wait here." The kid walks a short distance into the forest.

"Not like I can go anywhere right now," Cassia mutters. She nods at the others in his party, who are standing around awkwardly.

"'Sup." One of them nods back.

"Curious what your friend's doing."

He shrugs. "He's always doing shit like this."

They hear the crunching of leaves under his feet before they see him, walking out of the trees with a waist high and mildly twisted stick. He hands it to her. "Use this. It'll let you take some of the weight off the leg while still walking."

"Thanks," she says, marveling at how helpful this young man has proven to be. She thinks then of how the people back home turned their backs on her and Sophie, of how alone they felt facing the illness with only Haris and themselves; and of how supported she feels now, by this stranger who has gone out of his way to help her.

She leans on the stick as she stands upright and, surprisingly, it works. She thinks she can hike so long as she puts the weight of her right side on the stick instead of her leg.

"No problem. See you at the top!"

He and the rest of his friends start walking up, faster than she can hike. Especially now. Luckily, she gave herself plenty of time to make it, or so she hopes. Hand on the stick, she pushes herself up the hill, boots crunching on dry pine needles. The next problem she'll need to solve is what will she sacrifice, since she couldn't buy more than the one goat. But no use lamenting what isn't. Luckily, she brought bird seed, hoping that might attract a bird or a squirrel. It still might. But what if it doesn't? She turns the problem over and over in her head, worrying at it like a kid with a loose tooth.

Chapter 12

A few hours later, Cassia's leg doesn't hurt anymore and so she is free to keep worrying at the problem of what to sacrifice. Every time she sees a bird or a red squirrel up in a tree, she contemplates whether she can catch it. But then she thinks, I can't carry a live bird or squirrel from here to the altar! And so she doesn't even try. She'll have to figure something out when she gets there.

Because she's so caught up in her worry, she's not watching where she's putting her feet. She sets the walking stick down on loose soil. Her left leg slides into a hole just big enough for her boot. She is so consumed with her thoughts that doesn't even notice. When she lifts up her right foot to turn around a bend, the walking stick slips and falls out of her grasp. Her left knee twists while her foot stays in place, stuck in the hole she put it in. There's a loud SNAP! like a dry twig underfoot. She feels the pop inside her knee as much as she hears it. She screams, fire tearing through her knee and up her leg. She collapses to the ground.

Howling, Cassia grabs at her knee. Even through her thick pants, she can already feel the swelling. She doesn't know what she did to it, as medical knowledge was never her interest. She tore something, she's fairly sure. She's crying now, from pain and from terror that she won't be able to make it the rest of the way.

She sits that way for some time, long enough that the sun has moved in the sky and the shadows are deeper. She whimpers as she lays there, caught up in the waves of pain.

Eventually, the pain begins to dull. Sitting there, with only an ache compared to the agony she'd experienced before, she attempts to psyche herself up for standing.

She breathes out. "I can do this. I probably did only a minor injury, if the pain is already fading. This will be fine." Grabbing the walking stick and placing it on firm ground this time, she breathes deeply one more time then hauls herself up. Favoring her left leg, she limps a few steps.

She almost falls again.

She gasps.

She stays upright.

Her teeth are clenched, her shoulder muscles bunched, but she takes a few more steps. Up the mountain, not down. She will not give up. This pain now is nothing compared to what it would be like to live without Sophie.

One positive thing about this injury is that she is no longer fretting over what to sacrifice, or how she'll catch the animal. All of her attention is spent on simply walking. Every step feels like she's a new sailor, stuck on a boat in the middle of a storm.

She turns the bend and there is the second altar. Small blessings indeed.

She can hear laughter. When she gets closer, the same group of twenty-somethings is there, goofing off. She halts. They were so helpful the first time she hurt herself. She doesn't want them to know it backfired and she's even worse off than before.

Sighing, she limps over. She hopes they won't notice she's using the stick on the opposite side now.

The kid who gave it to her sees her coming and calls out. "Hey, Not-Grandma! How's it going?"

"My name is Cassia. You might as well know my name." She purses her lips. Speaking is difficult. "I hate to kick you out, but I'm going to need that altar."

He turns around, looks at the kid laying on top of it in mock sacrifice, then turns back to her. "Right-o! I'm Jack. That's Fred there on the altar, James with the goofy look on his face, and Matthew tying his shoes. We'll get out of your way. But what are you going to sacrifice?"

"I was hoping to lure a bird with some birdseed."

"If you know some bird calls that'd work out," Jack says with a flip of his hair. "They're so tame up here that they're not scared of humans. But they won't go to just anyone."

"Oh." Her hopes crash to the ground like a bird with a broken wing. One more obstacle to overcome.

"I mean, I know a couple," Fred chimes in, hopping off the altar with the knees of a twenty-year-old. "I can teach you."

"I know a couple, too!" James says excitedly.

"Really? That'd be great. But... Well, are you sure you know them? I mean..." She's sure she sounds stilted, maybe even rude, but she can't muster much enthusiasm right now.

They laugh together. "It's cool. We went to this summer camp together one year. They made us do this so much, like twenty times a day, that it became ingrained in our heads."

"Oh. That's... Okay. Cool. Thanks for reassuring me."

"No prob. Come chill with us and we'll teach ya all we know." Two of the young men lead her to a copse of trees, and she follows, slowly. She watches the others go to a different copse and begin passing something between them to smoke. Well, that'll keep them entertained for a good while, she supposes.

Sitting down is a relief. Together they practice for about an hour, them teaching and her learning. As they do so, a number of confused birds flitter about them, trying to figure out why they hear mating calls but see no birds to mate with.

Cassia laughs in wonder. They will show up. She just has to make the right noises, and they'll come. She experiments with putting a few seeds in her hand and holding it out. A tiny black bird with fire-red breast feathers flies right to her and rests on her hand for a second, just long enough to grab the seeds in its beak.

"Thank you," she says to the young men. "You have no idea how much you have helped me."

"No problem," Fred says. He and James wander over to the other two.

She stands up and walks to the altar, leaning heavily on her walking stick. As she unclips her knife from her belt, she suddenly realizes there's a major problem she doesn't have a solution for – can she stand on her injured leg without the stick for support? She sets the knife down on the altar, leans the stick against it, and releases it. Timidly she puts a tiny bit more weight on her left leg, then a little more. It hurts, but she thinks she can bear it.

She then roots in her pack for the right herbs – this time, Centaury for its medicinal properties, Elecampane also for medicinal properties, and Mistletoe for calling forth Asclepius. She puts half her birdseed in her hand. She tries one of the new calls she learned, hoping. A blue jay lands on her outstretched hand and begins to eat. Quickly, she grabs it, then her knife, and slits its throat over the altar. She then crumbles the herbs into the blood and calls out to Asclepius,

"Oh, Mighty healer Asclepius,
I beseech thee to give me an audience,
Hear my Plea of Need,
I sacrifice this bird of blue to you,
And give you the herbs Centaury for medicine,
Elecampane for medicine,
And Mistletoe, your favored herb,
Oh, Mighty healer, I beseech thee with these offerings."

Again, the blood boils and steams, but quickly cools down. It might be her imagination, but she thinks it took longer to coagulate this time. Perhaps a sign that she's doing something right! She grabs her stick for much-needed support.

She hears someone shout, "WHOOP!"

She turns her head around to see the young men all watching her, their mouths agape in fascination, fists pumping the air.

"That was sick, yo!" Jack calls out, then comes running over to give her a high five. "We've never seen a Greek sacrifice before. The blood boiling was so awesome. Can you do it again?"

She laughs in surprise at his excitement. "No, it's kind of a one-time thing. I mean, I'll do it again tomorrow morning, and hopefully they'll grant me an audience with Asclepius..." She cleans the knife on a handful of leaves.

"Yo, why isn't your wife with you? In America the Gods require the sick person to be present."

Cassia sheaths the knife, not meeting his eyes. "She... She doesn't want to petition them. She feels like her time has come."

"And you're still here, like, fighting for her any way you can. That's fuckin' romantic, yo."

She laughs. "Yeah, I suppose. But that's not why I'm doing it... I can't do life without her is all."

"I hope I love someone like that someday." His voice hitches at the end. It's barely noticeable, not something his friends would pick up from where they are.

She squeezes his shoulder in reassurance. "You will, if you keep your heart open. It's what I tell my son, just keep your heart open and keep trying to find love, and it will find you."

"That's deep, man."

"Thanks. I'd love to talk more but I really should get going. I've got to make it to the summit by tomorrow morning at sunrise."

"Sure, don't let us keep you. She must be one hell of a lady for you to do all this for her."

"She is." With that, Cassia turns to begin hiking further up the mountain. But she doesn't make it. Instead, her knee gives out under her and she falls to the ground.

"Hey! You okay?" Jack comes to her, squatting down.

"Yeah, yeah. I'm fine." Beads of sweat trickle past her eye.

"You don't look so hot. Did that cramp come back?" His forehead creases with worry.

She looks closely at him, wondering if Haris would be this attentive to a strange old woman in the wilds. She then thinks of Haris coming every day, of tending to Sophie, bringing food and blankets and even helping her to the toilet when she herself was out of the house.

"Something like that."

"You're like my grandma. She never wants to admit when something's wrong. Tell me."

She looks harder at him. He's a good kid, she thinks, much like Haris. Both are rowdy and rambunctious, but have good hearts. She sighs. "I did something to my other knee. I don't know what. I think maybe I sprained it?"

"What happened?"

As she describes her injury, the furrow on his brow deepens. When she finishes, he says, "I think you either sprained or tore your ACL. That's bad, Cassia. We can help you get back to town." He motions to where his friends are. They're standing around roughhousing and teasing each other.

She shakes her head. "No. No, absolutely not. I can still walk. I need to do this. I'd rather lose my knee than my wife."

He watches her for a long time. He nods. "Okay. But I'm going to wrap your knee, at least. Give me your knife."

She hands it over.

He proceeds to carefully cut her pants leg just above the knee. He then tears the fabric into strips, which he uses to wrap her knee.

As he does so, she asks, "How do you know how to do this?"

"My father is a doctor. I tried to follow in his footsteps for a while. I realized it just wasn't for me. But I picked up some useful skills along the way."

"Well, my lucky day, I guess."

He finishes up. "There. Try and walk on that."

She hoists herself up using the walking stick and tests out her left leg. It does feel a bit more stable now. She nods, tears threatening the back of her eyes. "Thank you."

He shakes his head. "I do what I hope someone else would do for my grandma. That's all. I wish you luck on the rest of your journey, Cassia. As soon as you can, see a doctor." He walks back to his friends. They immediately begin to roast him.

As she moves away, listening to the easy camaraderie of the hikers, she thinks to herself what a simpler age that was, with one's life mostly in front instead of behind. It's not necessarily that she misses that time, though in a way she does. It's more that she wishes she'd cherished those times when they were happening, that she understood then how precious they were.

Oh well. At least she can cherish what she has now, if she can convince the Gods to give Sophie more time. She hikes her pack up and begins shuffling up the mountain.

She barely makes it to her planned stop, the last light of the day shining on the rock scramble that signifies the final leg of the climb. It's supposed to be the hardest part, and with her leg as it is now, she suspects that might be even more true.

Luckily, someone else camped here not too long ago and their fire ring is still intact. There's even enough wood piled up inside it. Cassia takes a deep breath, grateful for the small things that make life easier. She leans her stick up against a tree and sits down.

After dinner, she is utterly exhausted. It makes sense to settle in for the night, hopefully get more rest than the night before. Tomorrow, she will crest the hill and make her last sacrifice. If all goes as planned, she'll be granted an audience with Asclepius.

Chapter 13

Cassia finally approaches the summit of Mount Olympos – the tallest mountain in the Greek world. It has been a hard climb, even using her stick as much as possible. Eventually, it gets too steep and she has to crawl up, with her stick secured between her bag and her back.

Scrambling up the last of the steep gravelly incline, she finally crests the top of the mountain, panting, at the same moment the early winter sun does. She pulls out her stick and leans on it.

The sun's light reflects blindingly off the snow. She brings the rim of her hat down to shield her eyes, then stumbles over to sit on a small boulder. She dusts the snow off it first, not wanting wet pants. Even so, she shivers as she sits down.

Cassia pulls her pack around to her lap, rummaging for sustenance. "There you are," she whispers in triumph as she finds a pouch of trail mix.

Opening it, she begins to chew, ruminating on the scene in front of her. She is at the top of the world, in the clouds, as close to the Gods as one can get.

The ground is covered in a one-inch layer of pure white snow. In the center of a plateau is an altar, surrounded by ornate, ancient columns and strewn with remnants of previous rituals like the aftermath of a bachelor party. Though given that most of the remnants are animal entrails, it would have been a much gorier party than any bachelor would wish for.

Trail mix finished, she stands, takes her stick and walks through the columns. When she arrives at the altar, she bows her head in reverence. This is it – when she performs the final sacrifice, to see if this will all be worth it. It's only been days since she was home, but it feels longer. She thinks back to the last time she saw Sophie, who was begging her not to leave. Blue eyes filled with tears and her shoulders shook. And still, Cassia left her.

If Cassia doesn't make it back in time… Well, she can't think that way. It **has** to work.

She returns to her pack, resolve to get this done as quickly as possible renewed. Pulling the knife from the front of the pack, she sets it down on the altar. Then the sprigs of sage, thyme, and dill on the other side, and bird seed into her palm. She turns to the forest behind her, scanning the mountainside. Making a series of different birdcalls, she waits a few minutes in between each to see if any birds come out. After her fifth try, a bird does come – a puffed-up black bird with a white belly, chirping in response. Cassia holds her hand out, palm facing up and filled with bird seed, and calls again. The bird lands on her outstretched fingers and begins to eat. A tear rolls down Cassia's cheek.

"I'm sorry."

Her hand closes around the bird. She fumbles around to find the flesh under the feathers and holds the bird at arm's length. Picking up the knife, she narrowly misses her own fingers when she slices the bird's chest open. The blood drips onto the altar then runs in rivulets down to the white snow on the ground. She lets the knife fall into the snow.

In a loud, practiced voice, she calls out,

"Oh, mighty healer Asclepius,

I pray to thee and ask thee to grant me an audience."

She crumbles each herb into the blood as she speaks.

"I give thee sage for wisdom, thyme for time, and mistletoe as your favorite herb, steeped in the blood of this fine bird."

The blood begins to boil, steam rises from the altar, and the snow on the ground melts in a widening circle around her. Her fingers clench, anticipating, hoping. This is it! This is the—

The altar stops steaming, the snow stops melting, the blood stops boiling. "NO!" She cries out in anguish, slamming her palm down on the altar. She doesn't even feel the sting from her skin hitting stone. "No! You have to at least listen to me. You have to at least hear me out!"

There's no answer from the Gods.

She sobs.

"That Gods damned Magi must have lied, or not known what he was talking about. There's no other explanation." She did everything he said to do. She performed the other sacrifices at the altars along the way. She left Sophie behind for this, on his word.

Both palms bracing her on the altar, she burns with anger.

Through her tears, she sees the knife laying in the white snow. It gleams in the sunlight, the bird's blood smeared across the metal. Cassia holds her breath. If the blood of a bird isn't enough, could her own work?

Cassia carefully kneels down and picks up the knife, feeling the weight of the handle in her right hand. She cleans the blade on her pants. She gently touches the tip with her left index finger and draws a bead of blood. It's sharp – she knows because she sharpens all her blades herself. A sharp blade is safer than a dull one. But in this case, she thinks to use that sharpness on herself.

Hesitantly, she touches the tip of the blade to the palm of her left hand. Then, without further thought, she slashes open the skin, across the head line of her palm. The sharp blade tears through muscle and tendon, down to the bone. She grits her teeth through the pain and squeezes her hand shut, letting the blood pool on the altar. She's out of fresh herbs, the last of them already on the altar soaked in bird blood. But she doesn't care. She lets the blood drip onto the herbs.

"Asclepius!" she screams. "Hear me now! I sacrifice my own blood to gain an audience with you. HEAR ME!"

The blood boils, bubbling across the surface of the stone. She can smell the iron in her own blood. She holds her breath, hope creeping back into her heart.

A deep voice reverberates from behind, around, and within her. "Did you truly believe sacrificing a tiny bird would be enough to secure an audience? We needed a bit more than that."

"Tell me how much you need and I'll give it."

The next thing she knows, an electric bolt zings through her body, tautening all of her muscles and frying the tiny hairs on her arms.

Chapter 14

What feels like hours later, Cassia finds herself kneeling on a hard surface, the pain in her knee intense. Her eyes are closed against the electricity still crackling through her. She shudders, willing her body to stop shaking. It doesn't work, not right away. When she finally stops shaking, she feels the blood pooling around her hand. It reminds her of where she's been. She opens her eyes to see she's somewhere very different now. The floor in front of her holds a puddle of red blood on white marble. Wincing, she sits back, and looks down at her hand, dripping a lot of blood. Is there a punishment for bleeding on the floor of the Gods? Either way, she should probably bandage that, but with what?

She slowly stands up. When she looks around, she sees she is in the peristyle before a grand palace, marble and gold accents everywhere. Encircling the courtyard are twelve marble thrones, each unique and almost all of them empty. She knows none belong to Asclepius because he doesn't have a throne. The only occupant is sitting bolt upright on the center throne: a stern, bearded God in a white toga. She can guess who that is, and it's exactly who she didn't want to see. Standing behind him are two mortal boys, both only about eight years old. One holds a tray with food on it; the other stands at attention.

Zeus stares at the blood on his marble floor, then up at her, then her hand. He sighs heavily and aims a thunderbolt at her. She flinches, expecting this to be the end. But instead of dying, she only wishes she could – the pain in her hand is multiplied a hundredfold, searing and burning and twisting. She holds her hand up to see what is happening and moans at the sight. Her tendons and arteries and skin are literally expanding before her eyes. When the skin finally connects, a flaming red scar bisects her hand. She tries to close it but the pain stops her at about halfway. She'll be able to do some things with it, but not much. She lets her hand fall to her side and looks up at Zeus.

When he sees that she is no longer bleeding on his marble, he flicks his hand to the boy at attention, who quickly comes over, produces a towel from his pocket, and wipes it up. He looks up at her and shrugs, then retreats back to his post.

Speaking in surround sound while also seemingly inside her own head, Zeus finally deigns to speak. "What brings you here, o lowly mortal one?"

She drops back to one knee slowly, painfully, bowing her head. "I came to see Asclepius, my Lord. I did not intend to bother you with my triviality."

"And yet you have bothered me." He sounds bored by this, but his voice still seems to reverberate in her bones. "If you desire to see Asclepius, you will first need to do something for me."

"What would you have me do?" Outwardly, she sounds calm, but inwardly, she's screaming, 'Oh shit oh shit oh shit oh shit oh SHIT!'

He picks carelessly at the dirt under a fingernail. "I have been craving one of my wife's golden apples, but she is currently mad at me about something or other. I ask you to go to her garden and pick me an apple."

"Just one?"

"Yes, that's all. If you do this, I'll have my boy take you to Asclepius."

Cassia bows even lower, her heart sinking. Her knowledge of the past tells her this will be no easy task, for it is one that even Hercules passed off. But it doesn't matter, for she will do anything to save Sophie. "Of course, my Lord. Which way is it?"

"I'll use my magic to send you over there. When you have the apple, I'll bring you back."

"Thank you, my Lord. That will make this task easier."

"I don't do it for you. I want my apple."

Without further warning, another jolt of electricity zings through her body. Her muscles and skin go completely taut and immovable. As before, it lasts only a few seconds, but they are torturous.

After what feels longer than it was, she opens her eyes and finds herself in a lush garden with exotic flowers and trees and ferns and plants she's never seen before. She gasps at the beauty, overwhelmed by all there is to see. There is an orchard of every fruit tree she's ever seen, and mossy carpet underneath. There are fountains with eerily cherubic stone children pouring glittering water from vases. There is an area with orchids, another with irises, and a third with daffodils; the vibrant flowers seem to watch her. She sees benches strategically placed for sitting and enjoying the beauty. There are multiple winding paths leading away from her. How will she find a single apple tree amongst all this?

She thinks of Sophie, then, and what she would do. She'd probably wander amongst the plants and get herself lost, but in getting lost, she'd find the apple tree somehow. That's what used to happen when they'd go shopping, anyway; Sophie would wander off and find herself in the completely wrong part of the market but somehow find the exact thing they were needing.

With renewed determination, Cassia stands, wincing. Her walking stick was left behind when she was brought to Zeus. She will have no way to support her knee. She takes a deep breath and begins to wander, ever so slowly. It will take a long while to get lost, she fears, with how slow she can move.

And indeed, it's hours before she stumbles across a courtyard with a single, large tree in the middle of a lake of cobblestone. Golden apples hang from it, sparkling in the sunlight. She doesn't celebrate, though, for wrapped around the thick trunk is a massive green serpent with easily one hundred heads, all looking in different directions. Its teeth are bigger than her forearm. She backs up slowly, knowing she's been seen – all one hundred heads are hissing at her now. She bows deeply and, remembering her recent readings and her teachings as a child, speaks. "Hello, Great Serpent Ladon. I have heard tales of your prowess."

The hissing continues.

"I was sent by Zeus to collect an apple. I don't suppose you'd let me?"

"Why ssshould I?" he hisses.

She continues to speak with her head bowed. "I am here to try and save my wife. In order for Zeus to let me speak to Asclepius, he directed me to collect an apple for him, since he and Hera are fighting."

"What'sssss wrong with your wife?"

"She's dying. Among us humans we call it the freezing illness. She's slowly dying of hypothermia from the inside out."

"Ssssoundssss chilling."

"Indeed. Will you provide an apple, then?"

"None have tried to appeal to me with honesssty. All before you have tried to take by trickery or force. Like Hercules." His voice sours.

"Well, I'm an old human woman. I'm not about to try and fight you. And I have no trickery left in me. All I have is the truth."

"I like you. But if I let you have one, I will have to anssssswer to Hera, and I do not care to incur her wrath."

"Then perhaps I could speak with Hera?"

"Ssssshe will never let you have one if it'sssss for Zeussss."

"I would care to try, at least. I have spoken with her twice before and perhaps she'll remember me."

Two women walk into the Heraion hand-in-hand, nervous and oh-so young and beautiful. They look to each other, excited, anxious. Mostly excited. They approach the altar and the priestess standing there. Together they bow and present their offering of a calf, mooing behind them loudly. They speak in unison,

"*With this calf we ask that you bless our union today,*
Oh Mighty and Wondrous Hera,

And give us many years of wedded bliss together."

And surprising everyone in the temple, Hera herself walks out from behind the priestess, looking down at them – and truly looking down, for she has chosen to be magnificent in height and appearance, easily eight feet tall and just as elegant. She wears a polos crown upon her head and carries a staff with a lotus on top. Her face is unreadable – is she here to grant them their marriage or to smite them?

Chapter 15

Ladon hisses and it's like the sound carries in waves across the garden, across a courtyard, and into a grand palace. Somehow Cassia sees the hiss as though it is a physical thing, and she sees all the places it travels, until it arrives and rests in Hera's lap like a sibilant housecat. Then her vision snaps back to where her body is and she shakes her head as though that will help her orient.

Hera appears, staff in hand, in front of Cassia. She is exactly as Cassia remembers her – regal, matronly, distinguished. Hera wears a polos crown upon her wavy light brown hair and a pristine white toga. Her deep brown eyes narrow at Cassia. "I recognize you from somewhere."

Cassia kneels as low as she can before the pain becomes untenable. "I'd hoped you might, my Lady. I have beseeched you twice before, once to bless the union of my wife and I, and the second to help me welcome our son into this world."

Hera appraises Cassia. "Hm. Yes, I recall you now. You two appeared to be very much in love."

Cassia flushes and speaks quietly to the stone beneath her. "Thank you."

"Why are you here now? Are you no longer happy with your lady love?" There's a touch of scorn in Hera's voice.

"No, it's not that. My wife is dying, my Lady. I came to Olympos to beseech Asclepius, but Zeus found me first. He won't let me see Asclepius unless I bring him one of your apples. I asked Ladon to bring you here so I could ask you directly, instead of stealing one."

"And you think I will give you one?" Now there is definitely scorn in Hera's voice.

"I thought you might."

"What gives you such... *interesting* thoughts, little mortal?"

"You told me and my wife once that we would go to great lengths for each other. We have indeed, and I am now going to the greatest of lengths – to save my wife's life, possibly at the expense of my own, if needs be. If I am not able to speak to Asclepius, she will die." Cassia's throat closes up and fills with dread; then, she breathes out and can speak again. "While I'm sure you don't normally care about the petty lives of mortals such as us, I thought you might care to save hers, since we share a romance so unlike your own."

"What pride you have, o' lowly mortal. You presume to compare your romance to mine?"

"I have read the histories. Zeus is often promiscuous, against your wishes, and you are often a spurned woman. Or so I have heard." Cassia dares to raise her head a few inches, so she can look up and maybe see Hera's face. She sees Hera glowering down at her.

"You will watch what you say, mortal." She seems to grow in size, her voice strengthening and hardening. Soon she towers over Cassia, her shadow dark and ominous.

Cassia kneels back, though keeps her head down, and puts her hands up in surrender. "Just, I thought you might like to prove Zeus wrong. Him sending me here was really him trying to get rid of me. He didn't truly believe I'd be successful; what threat would a fifty-six-year-old mortal woman be against the great serpent Ladon?"

Hera does not shrink, but her voice softens a miniscule amount. "You claim that by giving him what he asked for, we'd actually be doing the opposite?"

Cassia nods vigorously. "Yes, I believe so. Do you really believe Zeus wants me, a mere mortal, to get what I want?"

"No, that'd be unlike him, to want to help a human with no clear benefit to himself." Hera ponders for a few minutes. She is suddenly normal height again, and her voice is somewhat compassionate (for her). "But it doesn't matter anyway."

"What are you talking about?"

"It's too late."

"**What's** too late?" Cassia speaks harshly, her own voice threaded with fear.

"You have no further business here." Hera snaps her fingers.

Cassia feels a course of energy run through her – not painful like Zeus' electricity, but shocking nonetheless. She is then flying over the landscape, back the way she came, down the mountain and through the city of Litochoro and then into Dion, through the back alleys and through an open window and finally, finally, she's back home, standing in the bedroom she shares with Sophie. The bed is made and Sophie is not in it. She fears the absence of Sophie in this room might consume her. Hera's words echo in her ears.

Panicked, Cassia limps out of the room, not feeling the searing pain in her knee because the searing pain in her chest is stronger. She stumbles straight into Haris. He looks exhausted and wrung out. His eyes are red and puffy. "Mitéra," he rasps out.

"Haris. Where's Mom?" She turns, opening the closet, as though Sophie might be hiding there. All she finds is their clothes. She walks inside, her hand reaching out to touch Sophie's favorite lace dress. Somehow, Cassia knows that Sophie is nowhere in the house.

"She died this morning." Haris chokes out the words.

"No. No, that can't be. I reached Olympos. I was about to save her. No." It's only been two days since she left. How could Sophie have deteriorated so quickly? Did more time pass on Olympos than she realized? Is it possible she could have made the journey in one day? What could she have done differently?

Haris' voice breaks through her thoughts. "She told me..." He pauses to swallow his sob. "She told me to tell you she loves you eternally."

"No..." Cassia crumples like a used tissue, collapsing into herself on the floor. The tear in her knee feels like it's on fire. She pulls at her hair with her right hand. She sobs. Was she wrong to go? No, there was no other choice! "No! No, no, no!"

Haris sits down next to her and puts a hand on her back. She collapses into his embrace. Their tears bleed together as they hold each other.

She sobs and sobs until her insides are turned inside out. A need to see Sophie overtakes her. She pulls back and looks up at him. "Where is her body?"

"I've laid her out in the front room. On... Well, the only spot was on our table." He wipes his eyes. "I haven't... Well, I didn't know if I should wash her, or if I should find a woman to do it, since you weren't here."

Slowly, like a much older woman than she is, Cassia unfolds herself and shuffles into the kitchen. There, on the wooden table they'd picked out so many years before, the one they played games on and ate meals at and did science projects on, lays her beloved, eyes closed. Dead. Her beloved is dead and she wasn't here for it and oh my God, how will she forgive herself? She was so consumed with saving her that she lost everything instead.

Cassia sits down at the table, folds her arms on top, and then lays her head down just right so that she can see Sophie's face. She's beautiful even in death. "What could I have done differently to save you? How could I have moved faster? Oh, if only I'd known about that Magi weeks ago."

She is so lost in thought, trying to solve the problem of what she did wrong, that she doesn't notice the passage of time. Haris comes in and gently touches her shoulder. "Mitéra, we need to wash Mom."

Groggily, even though she wasn't asleep but lost in thought, she nods. Her bones creak as she pushes herself up out of the chair. She braces herself against the table, trying to get ready for this step. "Get me a bowl of warm water and towels."

Haris returns quickly, too fast for her to be ready. But it doesn't matter. He's right, this needs to be done so that Sophie can safely cross to the other side. Carefully, lovingly, Cassia unwraps Sophie from all her layers. When she finally touches skin, it's warm, almost like Sophie is still alive. Glancing at her face to make sure, she continues removing layers. Soon, her lover is naked on the table. It is a sight that Cassia has never wanted to see.

She takes a towel and dips it into the warm water – warm because Sophie always hated cold water, and even in death Cassia tries to accommodate her. Tenderly, she towels down Sophie's body. Each inch, each limb and stretch of skin, breaks her a little more.

Finally done, she turns to find Haris watching her. Tears are streaming down his face. She tries to smile at him, as though to say, "We'll get through this somehow," but her face doesn't cooperate. She nods instead.

At the closet, she again reaches for Sophie's favorite dress. It's not traditional white, but it's not like either one of them was ever traditional. The coral color will perfectly match Sophie's blonde hair. She slides the dress onto Sophie's body, buttoning the pearl buttons at the back. Her hair doesn't need much; it has always been easily managed, but she picks a handful of flowers from their garden and makes a floral wreath. She braids some hair around the wreath to keep it in place, pleased with herself. Sophie looks good. She would feel proud to meet her death as such.

Haris comes up next to her. "Is she ready?"

Cassia nods.

"Let's move her to the bed, then."

"Right." How will she ever sleep there again?

Together, they move her to the bed and arrange her on the pillows. She looks so peaceful. Cassia loses herself in the moment and startles when Haris touches her arm.

"I'll call for the procession, then."

"Already?" She looks down at her dead lover and wishes for just a little more time.

"We have to cremate her before her body begins to decompose. You know that. And you'll need to bring an offering. Don't forget."

"Yes, I know. Okay, be the responsible one. I'll sit here and pretend she's simply asleep..."

Before long, though, she gets up gingerly and walks into the kitchen. She will not let her grief get in the way of Sophie getting a proper send-off. Opening a cupboard by the sink, she finds a small ceramic jug in the back. They'd been saving this for something special. She ties it to her belt, as she won't have the hands to carry it.

Soon, an entourage of neighbors and friends enter their bedroom and offer their condolences.

"We're so sorry."

"I know you loved her deeply."

"You were always there for her."

"She was lucky to have you to rely on."

"At least she had you at the end."

At least she had you at the end.

At least she had you at the end.

At least she had you at the end.

But...

She didn't, did she? Sophie didn't have Cassia at the end, because Cassia was off on some grand quest.

Cassia breaks a little bit more, a few cracks in her heart widening and it feels as though lava is seeping out.

Eventually, everyone is there, everyone has spoken their sorrow for her, and they all look to her for the next step.

"Um... Find somewhere to stand around the body, and we'll all lift on three."

So, they do. Some must climb onto the big bed to reach Sophie. In all, six people surround her and collectively they carry her out of the room, down the stairs, and into the street. Cassia herself is unable to bear much of the burden, her knee still in bad shape, but this is not something she will leave wholly to others. As they walk, they sing the goös, each person singing a different version based on their memory of her, of the two of them, of the three of them. By the time they arrive at the crematorium, she feels deeply the bittersweetness of love.

A pyre has already been prepared: a wood frame of alternating logs surrounded by kindling. Who let the undertaker know they were coming? Was it Haris? Or do rumors spread that well?

They place Sophie's body on the pyre, still singing the goös but now also preparing their offerings and libations. Before anyone else can make their offering or libation, though, she must go first. She detaches the small jug she'd brought from her belt hook. It's filled with pomegranate mead, their favorite drink. She pours it out all the way around the pyre. After her, the rest of the mourners make their offerings. Haris goes last.

When they are all done, an attendant comes forth with a torch. He hands it to Cassia. She takes it in her right hand and stares dumbly at it, realizing all too late that now she is expected to light her lover on fire and watch her burn. She gags and tries to shove it back at the attendant, but he is already gone. Instead, Haris is there, from across the pyre, taking hold of the outstretched torch while simultaneously holding her up. His hand is gentle but firm over hers, and slowly, in fits and starts, they move toward the pyre. She almost gasps in relief when they finally touch the torch to the straw beneath Sophie's body. Her body shakes against Haris'. For the first time in her life, she actually feels old. Not just old but ancient.

Everyone moves back from the heat as it expands upward and out.

It would be beautiful, the fire, if it wasn't burning Sophie. Or perhaps it's because Sophie is the recipient that it is beautiful. Perhaps the beauty of Sophie is leaking out and tinging the fire itself. Either way, none can deny that it is mesmerizing.

About six hours later, Cassia and Haris are the only ones left. Sophie is mere ashes now upon the earth. Cassia squats down next to the pile. This close to the ashes she can see small bits of bone mixed in. The fire was suitably hot, then, to leave behind so little. Sophie should be well on her way to the afterlife. Perhaps they'll even see each other again, if the Fates be willing.

"Oh, Soph," she whispers. "I'm so sorry. I should have been there at the end. You were right, I risked too much, and I lost it all. I lost my last moments with you. If we meet in the afterlife, I can only hope you will forgive me."

Cassia sits down in the dirt, not caring that she'll get dirty. Even if she did care, standing by a burning pyre soiled her already. She scoops up some of the ash and lets it funnel from her hand into the tiny urn Sophie had picked out, when she'd first learned she was sick.

Haris squats next to her. "Come on, Mitéra. Let's get you home."

She nods numbly and lets him help her up.

On getting home and walking upstairs, Haris folds her into a hug. Leaning back, he asks, "Do you want me to stay the night? So you don't have to be alone?"

"When did you get so responsible and mature?" She asks, cupping his cheek with her good hand. "No, I'll be alright. I think I need some time alone now."

"Okay. I love you, and I know she loved you too."

Cassia nods. When he starts to turn away, she grabs his hand. He turns back. "Why aren't you mad at me? Please, Haris. Just be mad at me."

He smiles sadly. "I can't. I know you did what you did out of love. And so did Mom."

She shakes her head. "I did what I did out of fear, and pride, and... and... And selfishness! Love may have been part of it – no, no, you're right. It was part of it. Maybe even most of it. But it wasn't all of it."

He nods. "I know. Rest now, Mitéra. I'll be by in the morning."

After he leaves, she sits down at the kitchen table. Six or maybe seven hours ago, her lover lay here, dead. Just a month ago, they'd sat here, eating lunch or breakfast or something. She runs a hand over the smooth wood and wishes for just one more moment with Sophie.

"The closest thing I'll get to that, I suppose, is being where she last was alive. In bed. Perhaps... Perhaps I'll go to sleep, then, and perhaps I'll dream she's with me."

She hobbles into the bedroom and sits down on the edge of the bed. Her hand aches, where Zeus somewhat successfully healed it, and her knee throbs, but neither of those compare to the emptiness in her center. She curls up onto Sophie's side of the bed and sobs.

Chapter 16

W hen she wakes up, she's back in Hera's garden, lying on the cobblestones. She is in the same position as when she fell asleep, only it's much colder and harder here. She looks up and sees Hera above her, who looks down coldly, and Ladon, who looks at her with compassion.

"Well?" Hera asks.

Her voice is shredded. "She was right. I shouldn't have come. The risk was too great."

Hera nods once.

Cassia lays limply on the stone, everything seeming gray now where it once was vibrant and full of life. She wishes simply to go back to sleep. She raises her head, thinking perhaps to tell Hera off and ask to be left alone. But the words don't come, and she lays her head back down.

After several minutes, Hera kneels next to Cassia and speaks. "That was your future. A future you would have seen, if you hadn't learnt some humility. Let this be a lesson to you from now on. Gods don't like clever mortals."

"She—she's not dead?" A candle flame of hope lights up in her soul. She lifts her head with more strength, even propping herself up with her right arm.

"Not yet. But you still have trials to pass." From the folds of her robe, she pulls out Cassia's walking stick and hands it over. "This, though, might make things easier."

The flame of hope burns brighter, lighting up all the molecules of her body. She sits up. She puts her head in her hands. She can't get the image of Sophie's dead body out of her mind. The feel of her cold, dead hand. The light of the fire against the darkness of the night. But if that hasn't happened yet; there is still hope. She lifts her head. "And what of this trial? Will you grant me an apple, my Lady?"

"Yes, let's make Zeus keep his word. Ladon, if you please."

"With pleasssure, my Lady." And with that, Ladon parts his heads, making a clear path for Cassia to reach in and take an apple.

Cassia slowly stands up. The path before her, while clear, is still intimidating. Stepping closer to the giant snake goes against all her self-preservation instincts; even knowing Ladon will let her pass does not change the fact that he could kill her as easily as she might swat at a fly. She gingerly treads down the path and to the tree in the center. She reaches up to the lowest apple, its skin a glossy gold. When her hand barely closes around the smooth fruit, electricity spirals through her once again. The garden fades from view, the Goddess and many-headed snake replaced by a throne room and someone far more terrifying.

Chapter 17

"Well," Zeus says, taking the apple from her and biting into it, juice spraying out. The boy standing at attention hands him a towel, which he uses to wipe his face. He then hands the towel and the apple to his attendant and turns back to her. "I suppose I should send you to my grandson, then."

"That would be most appreciated, my Lord," Cassia attempts to fawn. It comes out weak. She feels weak, after the ordeal with Hera, and cannot summon the strength to appease this fickle God any longer.

Zeus doesn't seem to notice. He snaps his fingers and sparks fly.

A third mortal boy comes out of the shadows and hurries over. He bows deeply on approach. "Yes, my Lord?"

"Take this mortal to see my grandson, Asclepius."

"Yes, my Lord." He rises as he turns to her, then waves his hand to indicate that she follow. She is already moving.

"Thank you, my Lord," she says, bowing once more as she exits the hall.

She follows the boy through a maze of courtyards and hallways. She is certain she'd never make it out again on her own. Around every corner there is another marvel that if only she had more time, she'd relish studying. There are tapestries woven with shimmering thread, statues that appear to be made of light, and oversized amphora with fanciful depictions of the Gods. But her favorite are the gardens, even given her most recent experience in one. They brim with life and color. The grass is thick and she yearns to walk through with bare feet, to spend an afternoon picnicking with Sophia, to admire each and every bloom. She doesn't realize she's stopped moving until the boy tugs urgently on her sleeve. She tears her eyes away from the garden scene to look at him.

"It is best not to wander in this garden, lady. It is beautiful but treacherous."

"I'll take your word for it. Continue on, then."

After what seems like miles of treasures, so many that her mind is numb, they enter another grand hall, though not as grand as that of Zeus. In the center, standing on a bridge over a pond in which large silver fish swim, she sees a God that must be Asclepius. He looks so much like the statue back in Dion's temple that she jolts. But no, no statue could radiate godliness like this. He holds a golden rod with a silver snake wrapped around it in one hand, and the other rests lazily on the bridge railing. He looks up from his contemplations of the fish and looks annoyed by her presence.

His voice booms off the walls of the hall and inside the walls of her skull. "Iason, why have you brought me a mortal?"

"She did a ritual, sire, and Zeus answered. She asked for you by name."

"Hmph." His voice softens, enough that it doesn't echo inside her head. He peers at Cassia, then motions her forward. "Did you really come all this way for me to heal that?" He asks, derisively.

"What?" She looks down, to where he points, and realizes he means her knee. "No, I did not. That happened on the way here. I come on behalf of my wife. She has the freezing illness. It's too progressed for mortal doctors. I will do anything you ask, if only you will save her." She contemplates prostrating herself before him, wondering if it would help or not.

He shakes his head. "I cannot heal someone who is not present."

"That's what all the texts say, but I thought maybe..." She trails off, then starts again with more resolve. She must succeed here, or return to Sophie dead. "I thought that maybe if I could talk to you directly, you might know of a loophole. You are a powerful God, after all."

He sighs wearily and runs a hand through his grey hair. "Who is she? And where?"

"Sophie Vasiliadas. She resides in the town of Dion. Do you need more than that?"

"No, that is enough." He closes his eyes and his body goes rigid. After a few minutes, his eyes flash open and he looks at her sadly. "But unfortunately, while I could cure her, she will still die at the same time."

The news knocks the breath out of her. "How can that be?"

"She will die of another cause, one even I cannot see, because her fate line ends there. I cannot change the will of the Moirai."

Cassia moans, defeated, remembering Sophie's cold, dead hand. She staggers to a nearby bench and puts her head in her hands. She whispers, "After everything. I make it here and still..." She looks up at the God. "But then how do you save others? I have heard of your miracles."

He shrugs. "Their fate lines were not already cut. Perhaps the Moirai were working slow that day, or were busier than usual. Either way, if the fate line is cut, I can do nothing. She has one week left."

"No. If I don't succeed here, she will die without me. That's what Hera said."

He waves his hand dismissively. "Not my problem. Joseph, show her the way out."

The boy approaches her and tugs on her sleeve.

She stands slowly, devastated. But then she stops and turns back around. "Wait. Can I—Can I talk to the Moirai?"

"You can try. Dimitrios can take you." He indicates the boy who brought her there. "But they do not talk to many mortals and when they do, the price they exact is often steep."

"Joseph?" She asks in confusion, looking around to see if there is someone present that she didn't notice before. There isn't. She looks to the boy, who shrugs. "It doesn't matter. I will pay any price. Please heal her, my Lord, and I will find a way to lengthen her fate line."

"You will need to pay obeisance to my temple every year on this day. You will cut all of your hair and bring it to my temple, where you will burn it in my honor. Every year. Even if the Fates do not extend her line."

She touches her hair; it is soft and full. It is one of her few prides about her appearance, since she and Sophie sacrificed to bring Haris into being. But what is hair, compared to the life of your lover? "Yes, my Lord. Anything."

He closes his eyes again, his face motionless for several minutes. He opens his eyes and looks at her with curiosity. "Then good luck with the Moirai. I have done all I can for your wife."

She turns to go, then pauses once more. "Can I ask, my Lord..."

"What?" He responds, irritated. He was already looking at the fish but turned back to face her, clearly expecting a good reason to interrupt him again.

"Well, it's just... It was so easy for you to heal her. Why don't you simply destroy the disease itself, everywhere, so it does not plague the people?"

"It was the makings of a mortal, not a God. Thus, not my problem."

"A human created the disease? How?"

"That is what I said. By messing with magic. Now if there's nothing else?" He looks down at her.

"No, nothing else. Thank you for your time." She bows once more.

He turns back to the fish, dismissing her and Joseph or Dimitrios or whatever his name is.

Chapter 18

Haris sleeps, his bottom half in a chair, his top half slumped onto the bed at Sophie's feet. He's dressed in a tank top and shorts. On the bedside table are a handful of pill bottles and an empty bowl of soup. Sophie was asleep but something has woken her. Something shifting in her body. Like her blood is flowing again, not stagnant anymore. Her heart... She can feel her heart beating. She's HOT, oh so very hot and the blankets must come off now. "HARIS!" she yells.

He starts awake. "Is it... What? What's wrong?"

"Get these blankets off me."

"Why? Do you need to use the toilet?" He's already reaching under the bed for the bedpan they've been keeping there, since she stopped being able to walk to the bathroom.

"NO! Just get them off me! Now!"

"Okay, okay, Mom, I'm working on it." He pulls blanket after blanket off; she easily has twenty blankets on her. With the heater also set to 90 degrees, she's broiling.

After what feels like ten minutes, she's uncovered enough that she can wriggle out. She sits upright on the edge of the bed. "Get me a pin," she demands.

"Where do I find one?" He asks, hope and excitement trying to creep through.

"Look in my sewing basket."

He gets up and wanders out of the bedroom. Sophie hears him rummaging through her stuff. She doesn't care what mess he makes, only that he finds her a pin.

Finally, he walks back in, carrying a silver-headed pin, its tip gleaming in the morning sunlight. He hands it over. She suspends the needle above her left index finger, then looks up to Haris. For a weighted moment they stare at each other, both hoping and fearing to hope. The moment passes, and she quickly pricks her finger. Immediately red blood bubbles out. She exhales. "She did it."

Haris envelops her in a suffocating hug.

Sophie pushes him off. "She actually did it... I can't believe it. Yet again the Gods have smiled upon us. As usual, thanks to Cassia."

"Aren't you happy, Mom?" He pulls back and scans her face. He then pulls her back in to him.

Her voice is muffled against his shoulder. "I am overwhelmed. I was prepared to die, and now I'm not going to. It's a bit of a shock."

"Yeah," he says, but still not letting go of her.

"Now, let's hope that the cost was not too high."

"Was the cost high, with me?" He asks, finally letting her go, doubt creeping into his voice.

She smiles at him and puts her hand on his cheek. "You were worth it. But it was high indeed, for both of us."

Two beautiful women, one white and one brown, walk into a large marble temple together, holding hands. Between them they carry a basket with pomegranates and in the brown one's other hand is a bird cage with a dove inside. When they leave, they will carry nothing but their changed appearances, a dulling of eye color, an extra crook in a nose, unmanageable hair. But inside the womb of one is growing an exceptionally beautiful baby boy, and the other woman is missing a left pinky.

Chapter 19

The boy leads Cassia slowly down a dimly lit hallway. She keeps her eyes on the cobbled stones beneath their feet, not wanting to further injure her leg. The wall sconces are all on the verge of sputtering out, but they somehow keep going just enough for her to see the cobwebs in the recesses of the ceiling.

"So, is your name Iason, Joseph or Dimitrios?" she asks, trying to make conversation.

"Neither," he responds. "It's Georgios. None of the Gods can remember it."

"Oh."

He shrugs. "It's really okay. No one knowing my name is a small price to pay to live and work amongst the Gods."

"So, how did you get this job, then?"

Georgios stops, looks at her for a long moment, then sighs. He leans up against the wall, and in the sag of his shoulders she gets a glimpse of his true age. "I was a farmer, once, like my father and my father's father, and on and on, and my sons would have been too, if I'd had any. I don't know how long ago I lived, for I don't know how time works up here. But one day, the drudgery of my life... Of shoveling shit and killing the animals whose shit I shoveled... Well, it got to me. I prayed to the Gods, to give me another option. Zeus himself showed up and laid down the rules for me, if I chose to accept them. I took one look at my fields and knew I didn't want one more minute of being a farmer. So here I am, forever a young boy."

"Oh. Well that makes sense, then."

He nods, then pushes himself off the wall. "Come on, we have a ways to go yet, to get to the underworld."

She stops. "What?"

He turns to look at her impatiently. "Don't tell me you didn't know the Fates live in Hades."

She shrugs. "Okay, I won't."

He shakes his head. "Come along, there's a portal past the kitchen."

He brings her into said kitchen, the light bright in here compared to the hallway. It is open and airy, light streaming in from wide windows, with copper pots hanging from the ceiling and a large, man-sized oven in the center of the room. There is something cooking on the stove, a magicked spoon stirring it with no one standing over it. Her mouth waters instantly; she hasn't eaten since breakfast. Just about anything would smell enticing, but this is beyond that, beyond anything she's smelled before, and she thinks if she can only taste one bite, everything will be o—

The boy takes her by the hand and leads her away, snapping her out of the fog she was in. Whew. Who knows what punishment she would incur for eating the food of the Gods?

"You don't want to eat that. You would end up philosophizing for years, unable to think of anything but grand ideas."

She looks down in surprise at the young boy leading her, caught off guard despite herself by the mature words coming from a child's mouth. He doesn't notice her looking at him, or pretends not to. She shrugs her shoulders and chalks it up to Zeus being…. Well, Zeus.

"This way, now, before you find something else to tempt you." He turns a corner.

She isn't sure if he's playfully teasing or frustrated by her. She follows him.

She stops, yet again. She hasn't been paying attention for a while. Now, though, she can see that the walls are rough, not even brick but… She reaches out to touch one. It's hard-packed dirt? She looks to Georgios, who walks on oblivious to her confusion.

Cassia looks ahead, peering into the shadows. She can't see what she's about to walk into, but this is where Georgios says she must go, if she is to appeal to the Fates. Squaring her shoulders and breathing deeply, she walks forward and into the Underworld.

It is dark and shadowy here, and she can hear screaming far away. She wraps her arms around herself. Everything is gray and drab. She can barely even think of what color looked like, back on Earth. But there's no time to think, anyway – Georgios is continuing on without a break in stride. Catching up is a struggle not only because of her bad knee but the ground beneath is soft and sludgy. It's almost like walking through snot.

After she can breathe again, she asks, "Why didn't we have to cross the Styx?"

He doesn't look at her, his gaze focused on the path ahead. "That is the way for mortals. It was deemed important that there be a pathway between realms, for easy travel for the Gods. And, so it was made."

"Oh. That makes sense."

It's takes half as long as it feels like before they reach a round hovel set partially into the mountain behind it. It, too, is gray, though there are a few strands of green herbs in a window box below the sole window. The window glass is coated with dust, and only dim blobs can be made out through it.

He leads her inside. It is lit by flickering candles on every conceivable surface, and even some not so conceivable ones. Before her eyes can adjust, she feels a tug on her sleeve. She looks down at the boy, who bows, then departs. Cassia feels a pang of fear as she watches him leave. How will she return without him? Will she have to walk through the underworld alone?

Her eyes finally adjust, though, and she is reminded of her mission when she sees a large wooden table with three women perched around it. They must be the Moirai, also known as the Fates. On the table is a massive weaving loom, and in the loom is a tapestry. Even from across the room Cassia can see the sheer magnitude and beauty of it. There is a bundle of lustrous threads next to the tapestry, from which the women take to weave.

The smallest woman is elderly, so elderly it seems a miracle she's standing upright. She's so tiny and wrinkled she reminds Cassia of a raisin. She holds a pair of scissors poised over a shining thread like she was about to cut when Cassia walked in. This must be Atropos, the one who cuts the thread. Next to her is a woman dressed all in pearlescent white holding a smooth wooden measuring rod up to the thread. This is most likely Lachesi, the Fate who measures the thread. The third and final Fate is Clotho, the one who spins the thread. She is as young and beautiful as Atropos is old and wrinkled. She holds a spindle full of the iridescent thread. They all look at Cassia now, waiting, none of them smiling or seeming interested to see her.

She coughs. "Hi. Um. I'm here to ask if you could lengthen my wife's fate line."

"Why should we?" Atropos asks, her voice as withered as her body.

"Well. Um. Because... Because she's too young to die. She's only fifty-five! And because I love her, and we have a son together who needs her. And I need her."

"We can't just lengthen a line." Lachesi glowers.

"Pelops was resurrected after he was killed; you must have had a part in that."

Clotho nods. "But do you really wish a curse like his upon your wife?"

Cassia shudders. "Well then, what about Alcestus and Admetus?"

"Whose life would you sacrifice for hers? Your own? Your son's? That of a stranger?"

"My own. Take... Take some of my fate line and give it to her."

"Just some?" Clotho turns to investigate Cassia's line. "You have thirty-six years left. We would need that."

Cassia wraps her arms around herself. She would happily sacrifice all of her life for Sophie's, to never have to see the future Hera showed her, but that's not what Sophie would want. "Well, can't you take half for Sophie? That'd be eighteen years more for each of us. That seems like a good number."

Clotho shakes her head. "We demand a price. A sacrifice from you."

"Of what?"

Lachesi speaks up. "We would keep eighteen years of your life to ourselves. That leaves nine years for both of you. A good number."

Cassia stumbles. Only nine years left. Would that be enough? It'll have to be, nine years is better than nothing. She's fairly certain this is the best she's going to get. She may have been wrong to come, but now that she's here, she will do what she must to save Sophie. "I agree. Take nine years of my life and give it to her, and take eighteen for yourselves."

They bob their heads in unison, their eyes gleaming with greed. Clotho plucks a single thread from the bundle on the table. Cassia can feel the hands as though they are wrapped around her very soul. The lustrous thread shines like gold in the light. Lachesi measures the length with her rod, and it seems so short. They look to her one more time, Atropos' scissors positioned to cut. Is she really going to do this?

She thinks then of thirty-six years without Sophie – thirty-six years without her smile, her laughter, the inside jokes and the simple joy of being moms together. The answer is easy. Nine with her is far better than thirty-six without.

She nods her consent. Atropos cuts, and a chunk of thread falls away. She feels the life drain out of her like air from her lungs. She can't seem to take in a breath, only let it out. Did they only take what she agreed to? What if they took more? What if they don't give it to Sophie? What if—it stops suddenly, without warning, and she gasps for air. She puts a hand to her sternum, feeling for the intake of air, for the beating of her heart, for the signs of life. She breathes deeply, then looks to the Moirai.

They watch her, curious.

Atropos walks over gingerly and takes her elbow. "Come, my dear. Take a seat for a few minutes. It can be a bit shocking for mortals to die a little bit."

"Wait—I actually died a little bit?" Cassia takes the proffered chair.

Atropos scoffs. "What, did you think you wouldn't feel anything, that it'd be easy? If it was easy anyone would do it. It takes strength to withstand that, let alone to be willing to try."

"I could actually have died... fully?"

"The shock of your life vacating your body like that could have killed you, yes."

"You didn't tell me that," she says with a glare.

Atropos laughs. "We thought you knew. The cost of bargaining with the Fates can be your life."

Clotho passes her a mug with a deep red liquid in it. Cassia looks questioningly.

"Just some wine," Clotho answers. "Don't worry, we wouldn't give you anything that would interfere with your fate line."

Cassia takes a sip. It's sweet and rich in flavor but not too strongly tannic. Just the way she likes it. "But my dying would have affected my fate line."

Lachesi puts her hand on Cassia's arm. "And we would have known if that would happen. We have control over everyone's fate. Really you were in no danger; my sisters just like to be dramatic."

Cassia grimaces. "Um, so we both have nine years? To the day?"

Atropos shakes her head. "No. We can't tell you what day. That would fry your brain."

"Oh. Pleasant. And I'm assuming you also can't tell me of what?"

"Correct."

"I think I'm ready to go. Can you return me, or will I need to ask Zeus for another favor? I'd really rather not. I'm quite ready to go home, not on some other quest he might have."

Lachesi nods. "We can return you to the top of the mountain, if you're ready."

"The sooner I go back, the sooner I get to see my wife again. I'm ready."

"Then prepare yourself for this."

Chapter 20

Sophie is standing at the kitchen sink, washing up from dinner. Haris left not too long ago. They spent a full day together at the market and then making dinner. They had done much of that in the last six days together since she was healed, waiting for Cassia to come home. Sophie has been trying not to worry, that perhaps time on Mount Olympos passes differently. Perhaps Cassia is still in the middle of her journey, even though Sophie is herself already cured.

To distract herself, she hums a kantada, the same one Cassia was singing all those weeks before when she was making the bed, before all this drama happened.

When the window shutters slam open, she pauses in her humming and drops a ceramic plate. A gust of wind that smells exactly like Cassia rushes in. She breathes deeply without meaning to, and the force of the wind knocks her onto her rear. Still, she breathes in, deeper, deeper, deeper, until she doesn't know how, or if, her lungs can take it all. When it finally stops, she feels a little like a balloon that got blown up too much, and she suspects she'll be waiting to pop for quite some time. And she will – she'll be waiting to pop until the moment Cassia comes in the front door again.

She stands up and brushes herself off, looking around hesitantly. She feels like Cassia was here, right here, holding her, but she knows that's ridiculous. She walks down to the front door and opens it, just in case. She finds a moonlit night. The glow of the moon reveals no lover walking up to her front door. She exhales heavily. She shuts the door and walks back upstairs.

She walks to the sink to see if the plate shattered when she dropped it. It didn't. Seeing the plate, whole and perfect, resting in the sink, she realizes that whatever that was, it signifies that everything is back the way it was. This whole thing started with a shattered baking pan and it ends with a not-shattered plate. Somewhat fitting, she feels.

"But..." she whispers. "I was already healed last week. So what exactly was **that?**"

Chapter 21

Travelling by the power of the Fates is even worse than travelling by Zeus' power. Rather than a lightning bolt zinging through her body, she plummets through a tunnel displaying all of her worst memories. Getting teased in school. Finding out the news about her parents' tram accident. The devastated way Sophie looked when she left her three days ago. And worst of all, the future as predicted by Hera. All the moments she never wants to relive but has to if she wants to get back to Sophie.

She gasps for air.

She finds herself back on Mount Olympos, on hands and knees in the snow, with her left shin feeling like it's going to freeze off. She looks down and remembers that Jack cut her pants to just above her knee. She finds her walking stick in the snow next to her and stands up.

Her hands are covered in snow, painfully red. How had she not noticed that sooner? "Dammit."

She scrapes the snow off by rubbing her hands on her pants, then shoves one hand in a pocket while the other clutches the walking stick. Luckily her pants are still mostly dry, at least on the inside. Cassia limps over to the altar and finds her pack. Unfortunately, it's been torn open by what look like sharp claws. Raccoons, probably. She rifles through and moans in frustration. All her food is gone, but luckily they didn't care about her water. She shakes her head, like she's shaking off the worry. "I'll deal with that later."

She looks up to the sky; over half the day is gone. Though what day she doesn't know; does time pass the same with the Gods as amongst mortals? This isn't something covered in the histories.

Unless Zeus thought to punish her, she chooses to assume that time passed normally. Which makes this the same day she ascended the summit. But either way, she should still get moving quickly so she can find a place to sleep before it gets dark and cold. Colder, that is.

Climbing down the rock scramble is far scarier than going up, especially with her knee. Every jolt sends a fresh wave of nausea through her whole body and she fears she'll fall. The cold sunlight beats down on the rocks and on her, showing clearly the path down. She shudders at the thought of falling, then takes another careful step. When it gets even steeper, she scoots down on her butt, trusting that her fate line is fated to last another nine years. Still, no point in tempting them.

Finally at the bottom of the rock scramble, Cassia breathes a sigh of relief. She stops at her campsite from the previous night – is it the previous night? Again, she wonders how much time really passed while she was in Olympos. On the top of the mountain, it had seemed like no time at all. But here, at that last campsite, it seems like much longer. The fire is buried, the rocks shifted, leaves scattered all over the ground.

She ponders whether she should camp there or make it to the refuge. The desire to see Sophie as soon as possible has her deciding to push herself. She doesn't care if it causes permanent damage to her knee, if it means she'll get to see Sophie sooner.

She resumes walking. The way down is much easier than the way up.

She makes it to the refuge after sunset, the dim light from the full moon making everything softer. Wait – the moon is full. That must mean that... has a week gone by, then, since she traveled to the summit? She touches the top of her head, like she's trying to stop her brain from exploding. Emotionally it felt like years, yes, but in terms of time it hasn't felt as long as a week.

People are milling about the refuge tonight, and she suspects there's some kind of event with the full moon. Not wanting to interact with people, Cassia bypasses the refuge and goes straight to her camp from... well, a week ago, perhaps. There's still a ring of stones from her previous fire, thankfully – this campsite is even better preserved than the other one. Probably due to the lack of snow. She sends a prayer in thanks that all she needs to do is collect sticks for kindling. She doesn't know if she could do more than that, with the condition of her leg.

She will, however, have to figure out dinner, as she is somehow all out of trail mix and dried meat. Cassia looks over to the people at the refuge, the ones wandering about with glasses of wine in hand. She could ask them for help, and they'd likely give it, but... Well, what did Hera say about humans with too much pride? What if this is yet another test?

That settles it, then. If it's another test, she won't fail. She'll find food on her own. How she will do that with a gimp leg by the light of the moon with no weapon, she doesn't know, but she's going to try. She hobbles into the forest quietly.

She's not sure what she's hoping for. A rabbit on its last breath just waiting for her to show up and cook it? Yeah, like that's going to happen. If only she'd brought that bow and quiver. Not that she was ever a good shot on the best of days, but it would have given her a chance at least.

She walks into a clearing lit by the full moon. Everything around her is rimmed by an ethereal yellow glow. She turns her head in awe. "Wow..." she whispers, simply looking upwards.

Minutes or maybe even hours pass; she will swear, for the remaining years of her life, that she could even see galaxies amongst the stars above. When she hears leaves rustling, she expects to look down and find a fairy or a nymph. Though she doesn't know if fairies exist... But what she finds looking back at her is a rust-red fox, its head cocked to one side and its ears at attention.

"Hi," she says and waves. What exactly does one say when they meet a fox in a magical clearing at night under a full moon?

The fox doesn't move, only continues to stare at her.

Her shoulders drop and she slumps against a tree. "Right. I shouldn't have expected you to be able to talk. It's just... Well, I've come so far and done so much and now I'm... Well, I'm really hungry. And I'm all out of food. I was hoping maybe... I don't know. Maybe I'd find a berry bush? And it wouldn't be poisonous and give me the runs, that is. Anyway, I don't know why I'm spilling this to you. I doubt you can understand me."

The fox stares at her for a moment longer, then scampers off.

"Figures," she mutters.

Before she can do anything else, like wander around and find another magical clearing, a white rabbit runs out of the underbrush, followed closely by the fox. The fox pounces and grabs the rabbit by its neck. He shakes it a few times, then drops it at her feet, dead, its blood stark against the white fur. The fox cocks his head at her, eyes questioning. She nods once. The fox turns and lazily wanders off.

"Well. I guess he did understand me, after all."

While the fire gets going, Cassia skins and cleans the rabbit, fumbling through the process as she tries again to remember her father's teachings. Once she feels it's good enough, she creates a spit over her fire and slowly roasts the rabbit. She has no herbs to rub in, but she's hungry enough that it'll taste delicious anyway. She falls into a pseudo trance watching the fire, the way it flickers reminding her of candlelit dinners with Sophie.

When the smell of the rabbit hits her nose, she comes back to reality. Her stomach growls, and she doesn't care if it's fully cooked – it's cooked enough. She pulls it off the spit. The meat is tender and falls right off the bone. After not eating for what feels like days, she devours it quickly. Even without spices, it's satisfying.

Chapter 22

Three days later, Cassia stands outside the front door and revels in the sights and sounds. She hears Sophie singing that kantada from weeks before. It's still popular on the radio, for she heard it streaming out of the windows in Litochoro and again in Dion. It's belittling to realize that despite all the drama she has gone through, the rest of the world has continued on, unaware.

Inside, she sees a coat thrown on the floor, and pairs of shoes on opposite ends of the mud room from each other. She sighs and shakes her head. If she had any doubt that Sophie was doing better, it's the mess that she leaves everywhere that confirms it.

She leans her walking stick up against the wall, then her pack, the hatchet clanging on the wood floor. She cringes at the sound. She cocks her head to hear if Sophie has stopped singing, and when the song continues, she hangs up her jacket, and finally shucks her boots. She doesn't bother putting any of it away; she'll get to that eventually (several days, it will turn out. That's how long it takes for them to want to leave the house). She limps slowly upstairs on very stinky wool socks, then stands in the doorway, watching as Sophie flits around the kitchen like a fairy. She's singing loudly and badly, but Cassia doesn't care; she thinks Sophie has never looked more alive or more beautiful.

When Sophie turns and sees Cassia standing there, she drops the spoon she's been using as a microphone and simply stares, drinking the other woman in like water after days in the desert.

"You did it," Sophie whispers.

"I did. And I came back," Cassia responds, gently.

"Oh!" Sophie exhales and runs to Cassia, leaping into her arms like they are young again.

In Cassia's mind, a litany of 'I almost lost you' repeats, and she squeezes tighter. She feared she'd never hold her again.

After a solid ten minutes holding each other, Sophie pulls back and looks sternly at Cassia. "Tell me everything," she says. "Don't you dare keep anything back."

And Cassia does.

Later, Sophie and Cassia lay in bed, naked, wrapped around each other. The white sheets are tangled at their feet. Moonlight streams in through the window slats, reflecting off Cassia's eyes as she looks at Sophie.

"How could you?" Sophie whispers.

"I truly thought everything would be alright, that the price would be easy to bear. I was wrong, but not so wrong as to have failed."

"But they took... They took half of your remaining life. And then gave me half of what was left. That left barely any for you."

"It wouldn't have been any life, without you. You are my everything."

"What about Haris?"

"What about him? Doesn't he deserve both his mothers? I did it for him, too."

"I don't know if I can forgive you."

"I don't need you to. I just need you to live."

"And if I said I couldn't live with you anymore, knowing what you did? If I can't bear the responsibility of stealing your life, even though it wasn't my choice?"

Cassia pauses for a long time, and when she finally speaks, her voice is thick like the air on a hot summer day. "It would still have been worth it, to know you're alive somewhere, even if it's not with me. Isn't that part of loving someone, wanting them to be alive and happy?"

"Isn't part of loving also letting go? And trusting them? I told you I was at peace with my fate."

"I'm willing to let you go. I will never be willing to let you die."

Sophie sighs and rests her head on Cassia's chest. "I don't want you to die, either. Nine years doesn't feel nearly long enough."

"But it's nine years we'll have together. Nine more years to prepare Haris, maybe even see him find his way, to find his partner and his passion in life. Nine more years could see us grandmothers, even! A lot can happen in nine years."

Sophie shakes her head. "I have never been able to stay mad at you. Tell me again. We both die at the same time, but you don't know of what?"

"Yes, that's what the Moirai told me. They said knowing too much could overload my brain. It is bad enough that I know the time period."

Sophie trails her fingers along Cassia's bare skin, following the path of freckles from her belly button down. "Well, let's make the most of the time we have, then."

About the Author

Taylor Metzler currently lives in northern California with her family and cats (and some other pets that need not be mentioned, but we did anyway). She's been writing since adolescence, and reading more than is healthy for most people. She graduated with a degree in anthropology with an emphasis in museum studies and a minor in art history, none of which she uses. She enjoys such boring hobbies as crocheting and baking things that are far too tasty to be safe.

Read more at https://www.taylormetzler.com.